THE DEVIL SHE DREW

THE
DEVIL
SHE
DREW

A NOVELLA

NATE FERREIRA

Paperback ISBN: 978-1-7373142-0-2
EPUB ISBN: 978-1-7373142-1-9
LCCN: 2021910962

Typesetting: Stewart A. Williams | stewartwilliamsdesign.com

www.nateferreira.info

FOR MANDY

"It is not only the ratio of pleasure to pain that determines the quality of a life, but also the sheer quantity of pain. Once a certain threshold of pain is passed, no amount of pleasure can compensate for it."

—DAVID BENATAR

ONE

L AUREN BEVILL WAS ALONE the day it began. And hungry. Snow had soaked into her striped leggings, and the hem of her dress was cold and wet. Although she'd rolled down the long pink sleeves of her undershirt, the snow had managed to sneak up the pilling fabric.

Her dress was a finely stitched gray rabbit. Its paws were shallow pockets, and ears flapped near her shoulders. It had passed between manicured hands at last week's Young Midwest Mothers get-together, followed by rephrased comments of cuteness. And still, details would be disremembered in the unofficial police report.

Puffs of moisture popped into the air as Lauren carved her favorite creature, her late dog—a boxer named Roark—into the hard soil. Despite the jagged curves and chopped edges, she had developed him quite well before she began to tire.

Missing children had become common in Luso County. Perhaps something going terribly wrong should have been expected. As it happened, the Bevills—all of New Sagres City really—were ill prepared.

A grumble. Lauren dropped the small stick, held her stomach, brushed the collecting snow from her dress, and picked it up again.

Leaden clouds paused over the patchy yard. Dad wouldn't be back before dark. The routine wait allowed the adroit artist patience for detail. The floppy ears. His droopy eyes and animated brows. The cone on the top of his head.

Permission to go inside the mossy mobile home before the clouds made good on their threat seemed increasingly unlikely. The looming trees bowed in waves, their spikes setting mists of snow gliding from the edge of the woods toward the little girl.

She constricted. All but her shaky drawing hand. She tried to distract herself from the biting cold by focusing on her project.

A loud crack.

Then it stopped. Like an interrupted lightning bolt.

The echo carried beyond the lake to the south, where birds plunged and ripples scattered from their predatory dips.

Snow crunched. Not near the lake to her back. Lauren's eyes crawled across the treeline before her to the trunk of a spruce some forty feet ahead.

A glanced atrocity and her feet kicked from her cross-legged seating, scattering her canvas. Her hands slipped, in an attempt to brace herself on the slick snow and push herself up to stand.

Bloodied eyes. Or were they just sockets? A broken jaw hung open, and blood oozed down its neck.

And there was a second presence, someone far less marred. A mannish figure who held the sufferer; carried it, steadying its battered head, which shook in subtle spasms.

A good time to leave.

The next sound wasn't a moan from the bludgeoned or an effort-born grunt from the man who carried it. As Lauren squeezed her eyes, pain shot from her tailbone up her spine. When she looked up from her clumsy misstep, the tree sat alone. A red streak ran down its trunk, forming a puddle at its base.

The silence was commanding enough to emphasize the snowflakes that whisked past her face and tickled her nose. *Don't scratch. Don't move.* She waited: still only fallen branches and thick roughage past the woods' border.

The house. She could break the rules.

No, the punishment would be worse than the gored face if she didn't remain outside. Worse than the throbbing ache that lingered from her slip. A sufficient deterrent from interrupting Mom's visit with her handsome friend—and from leaving her lookout post and running the risk of ruining the mendacious game of which parent would greet the other first. A game Mom wasn't keen on losing.

Besides, no one would believe her. *She* didn't believe her. Her mind had played a trick. That was it. But the blood had looked real enough. It pooled and puddled into the slushy snow.

Just a peek. A tiptoe to check its authenticity.

Suddenly a squeal pierced the air from deep in the woods. Much deeper than the tree tagged in smeared handprints. Her investigation was aborted before it began.

Thin, frail fingers gripped the splattered base of the tree. Broken nails splintered the brittle bits and dug into the more resilient grooves. Half a forearm protruded. Dark and shiny, like it was draped in oil. Muscles contracted behind tight, dehydrated skin.

Lauren squinted, her eyes flashing over its arm. Lying on the ground, it shivered. The crippled thing was now hauntingly alone, gripping the trunk for stability and exposing its face again. Lauren's fear concealed the details. But the hurt thing was a woman; that much Lauren could make out. Blood swathed her twisted form.

That was enough incentive for a run. She peeked over her shoulder as one foot lunged in front of the other. A swivel, just enough to catch the mangled woman crawling from the woods before her sight went dark.

The pang in Lauren's head made tough work of opening her eyes to the clouds above. An angry, frigid ground bit at her back and buttocks. The concrete base of the carport stung her spine. Rocks shifted under her palms. She pushed up fast enough for her head to spin.

Her mother's laugh bubbled from inside the house; she clearly wasn't burdened with concern for the sub-thirty-degree weather or the desire to check on her unsupervised child. The giggled accompaniment made Lauren's headache worse.

A luxury SUV was parked in the carport. The stars in her vision had begun to flee to the sides of her big, green eyes.

The woman at the tree was gone. Trails of blood were smeared across the ground but hadn't made it far past the treeline.

Lauren doddered to the living-room window and braced her bluing hands on the yellow-green walls.

Just a quick peek. She'd be careful.

Mrs. Bevill stammered for words but quickly surrendered with broken chuckles. Her friend's tie was loosened but still hung from his neck, and Mrs. Bevill pulled at it playfully. Sharply. His blazer lay crumpled on the ottoman.

He chased her around the furniture, tickling when her feeble attempts to escape failed.

Lauren had seen enough of her mother's guest, or rather *hadn't* seen enough of her own guests, un-invited as they were. Exasperated, she turned and slumped, her back to the house.

Mildew pressed against her, smearing into the back of her dress with each heave for breath. Her eyes again scrambled to the treeline. Her head throbbed from the collision, and she was sure the carport's metal support had left its stamp on her.

The squeal again. This time a pleading, an-guished screech.

It could have been an animal. Couldn't it? A per-son? Natalia Monts had gone missing in the woods a few months ago. And Janelle Simmons, years be-fore they had moved here. Something, someone could be hurt.

Lauren's eyes widened as a figure appeared.

"Daddy?" The first call possessed more con-viction than the second. Fear, certainly. But the second only started and had trailed off with the first "D." By the first call, she knew something was wrong. By the second, she noticed the bloody mask underneath a hood worn by a tall, approaching man. His curled fingers dripped with blood. The mangled woman wasn't at his side or dangling from his arms. Somehow his isolation made it worse.

Blood clung to his long arms and tattered clothing.

Although tears obscured her vision, she knew it was time to run. She had planned to run away before, played it over in her head. When the punishments became too grueling. When she felt she couldn't take another night of her parents' screaming. No scenario, however, had a man with a bloody mask.

She pushed from the house and bolted to the forest line opposite the bloody trunk. Just a bit closer to the lake. Just a bit farther from the lanky, tall man. Loose gravel hid under the snow on the driveway. It shifted and moved, yet failed to trip the sprinting girl.

The treeline was dim and warning. Lauren peeked inside. The stirring gray of the brush and the glint of unrest weren't enough to dissuade her. Just a quick glance back.

He was gone.

She wasn't going to make sure.

She grasped a branch to steady her first step

into the woods, dismantling a partition she'd never dared to attempt until now. But breaking the rules felt less significant than she had anticipated. On the nights she had dreamt of escaping, it was not only the anticipation of punishments if she were caught but also the threatening woods that had thwarted her plans.

In fact, the severity of the consequences sure to follow didn't hit her until she had sprinted far enough into the woods to fear she was lost.

By then, the panoramic hell that projected from every part of the woods had become ubiquitous. Even so, and despite her contempt for the unknown—a formidable opponent to her audaciousness for as long as she could remember—she pressed on. She had become more enticed by a sure time than an exciting one, even one that held the likelihood of violence.

Unbefitting of a girl dressed in over half a decade of welts, scars, and distinguishing marks, sure. But better the belt-wielding devil you know, perhaps.

The forest's obscurity reminded her how out of character her behavior was. And how she wouldn't soon go to sleep without a nightlight.

She noted how little the few animals surrounding her comforted her. Usually, just watching the black squirrels launch from tree to tree and duck under shrubbery here and there provided among her only sources of peace.

She had no time for them now. No time for their two-footed stances, their big-eyed intrigue. Undoubtedly they had an easier time of it. Of surviving the woods. And she couldn't relate to them anymore. For a moment, she resented them.

The cheap, short-cut repairs had been made in a hurry. A shed, deep in the woods. Different occupants had attempted to salvage it many times since its original construction nearly seventy years before Mr. Bevill had claimed it. Yet none seemed to undo the makeshift restorations attempted before him. Instead, each had been made on top of the other like a bandage for a bandage.

And each with less assiduity than the last. The layered roof repairs were topped with moss like an emerald parasite corroding in uneven patches, swelling the burden of the fatigued, bowed walls.

Broken glass and window frames leaned against its side, their decomposition mourning long years of servitude to the shed. Crumbled twigs and thistles bordered its base.

The door was cracked open.

Lauren turned sideways and squeezed in without

touching it. Dust, mold, decay, and dirt covered everything. She spotted a stack of pocketknives now glued shut with corrosion. Several tools lay scattered across a wooden workbench.

A toilet kept the door of a small back room from opening fully. She poked her head inside. The room was clogged with trash and tools. A jackhammer leaned against the wall; rust from the leaky roof had painted it red-brown.

It was too quiet.

She mistrusted those peaceful, quiet feelings. The way she mistrusted the lack of an ache in her stomach now and again. Uncomfortable but discernible, familiar. With the forest repressed and hushed, she felt blind to its agenda. She knew, or perhaps thought she could guess, how horrible a thing could be lurking.

But she wanted to know, *had* to know. So in a way, had she asked for it? For the ripping and tearing that finally broke the silence, a racket of vibrations pushing through the cloudy window like the whine of a broken, falling tree?

Lauren stared, eyes fixed to the murky glass, and tiptoed toward it.

Insects fled, disrupted by a rare trespasser. Pressing a rag to the window, she breathed deeply. The air had a bad taste. Forced through the small space between her lips, transported on the backs of dusty granules. But breathing through her nose would be too loud, too difficult to control.

Frost and muck collected as the rag smeared across the window. Just enough to see.

When it came to exploration, Lauren had been able to limit herself to studying animals. Any more than that was too risky to find out what her parents would allow and what would enrage them. It was difficult enough with necessities; no sense testing for curiosity's sake.

But discovering what was on the other side of the window was about more than curiosity. More than the childish expeditions of a little adventurer.

Lauren strained her eyes in focus, caught a scene she wished she hadn't, and closed them.

She slid to a sitting position below the window, out of sight. The filth that had collected on the wall sponged into the mildew-painted cotton tail of her dress as she slid down.

She felt sick by the spectacle: a bony, craggy back bent over the meaty remains of...*something*. And the woman, the same wounded woman, lay not three feet from his side. It *had* to be the same woman.

Vibrating chills pronged her muscles. Squeezing her eyes shut didn't work. She could still see the tall man gripping the carcass in front of him. He was ripping its flesh, only showing care in the delicacy with which he placed the dripping strips of it onto the unconscious woman.

Squeezed in a ball, Lauren shook and clamped her hands tightly to her ears, until the sounds were as muted as she could force.

She waited.

Waited until the ripping had stopped. Until a loud screech was followed by heavy footsteps. Close at first. Then farther.

Her head inched to the windowsill. Webs stuck to her face and hands.

They were gone.

An accidental nudge upon her exit, and the shed door resumed its years-long post with a short, whining creak. But she didn't shrink from the barbarism; rather, she approached it. One slow step at a time, thundering in the quiet woodland.

Remnants of a carcass where the man had knelt. *A doggy?* The trees watched meticulously over her concern.

She squinted. Not a dog but a pig. Flesh hung sparsely to its coarse black fur. A panicked look still clung to its face. Not the most methodical butchery.

She'd never seen death. Not like this. Although she'd heard screams from the forest before. It must have been the hog's bellows that she'd heard earlier that day. It hadn't died quickly.

The memory of a belt sounded in her head.

The metal-clasp belt. The conclusive clank it made when Mr. Bevill set it on the dresser. It was the remembrance of successive throbs and the expectation of a reintroduction to the belt that snapped her from staring at the blood, which was strewn along the ground like spilled red tar.

A shallow creek wound twenty feet from the girl. Twenty feet closer to home. A slender red stream rode atop its surface, stretching like a fraying rope from one bank to the other and ineffectually trying to dissipate into it. Lauren looked from the winding streak of red to the carcass. Then back to the red stream. Was there no connection?

The smell had somehow stayed with her. Despite the cold breeze that heaved through the trees, the musky scent of rust and sawdust clung to her body, warning the woods of the intruder. The ground was too wet to keep her movements silent, so she lifted each step high and down again slowly. *Not quiet enough.*

She committed. In an instant she followed the slithering stream. Balancing across the slick tops of protruding rocks, she crossed the shallow creek. Congealed ruby guided her to its source.

She only truly caught control of her footing when she reached the other side and jumped from the untrustworthy rocks onto the slick snow, arms spread wide.

But not to another creature. A gray stone, a slate. No bigger than her mother's tablet, its edges coarse and jagged. Its surface was layered and imperfect like choppy ocean waves.

The encirclement surrounding it had become a crimson liquid. The bank was cracked and sunken like it was trying to pull the slate into it. Steam clung to an oozy mixture spilled from the slate's center and edges. Blood, from the look of it.

Lauren's skin tingled and tightened. The trees were stagnant; the animals had disappeared. The marks on her hamstrings twinged with a lean. She stretched for the metamorphic rock, confused by the blood. Intrigued perhaps. Ignorant enough to grasp it. A fine-grained and forewarning fossil.

When she retrieved it, she didn't feel its rough edges. Or the blood. She didn't feel she was in the woods at all. No, it was almost as if she was in her living room.

Not the mobile home but her old house. The big house. She sat cross-legged in front of the TV.

She couldn't remember what she was watching. But she remembered the juice, the guilty panic when it had spilled as she was pulled away.

She remembered distinct details, like how her bare heels went from being burned by carpet friction to feeling the cool kitchen tile. She remembered the force, the throb in her arm. How instantaneously she suffered a headache every time the back of her neck was struck.

She didn't want to remember any more.

Her eyes opened to the slate. To the shed and the needle-filled path that had led her there. A breath relaxed her muscles enough for her to move. Enough to remember the tall man. If not for his pursuit, she wouldn't have found the scary-looking rock.

She wouldn't have even left in the first place. She would've stayed in the yard. Would have explored some creatures and drawn. And she might've been allowed to go straight to bed.

The man with the nasty mask, the woman, the strange bleeding rock. None of it mattered if she couldn't prove it, if she couldn't justify absconding deep into the woods. Or even leaving the yard. Going anywhere without permission. Even if it was the first time. Why did she have to run?

The woods sat on a hill. Or perhaps the mobile home was in a valley. Either way, the transition from high to low ground was no good for running.

Lauren had scarcely a moment to review the mental draft of her adventures, hastily garnished with reassurances that she could have behaved no differently. Scarcely a moment to contemplate the punishment she'd select, if given the choice.

The run back seemed much shorter than the one into the woods yet more terrifying. More frightening than being chased by the tall man or hearing the screams or seeing the wounded lady. Perhaps it was the skyline. The pitiless, pale orange signaling her failure to abide by the rules and professing the severity of her punishment.

A quick detour. Yes. She had to hide it. She looked under the mobile home, past broken segments of the bottom board.

The smell of mothballs made her grimace.

A shadowy bundle made her jolt.

Wrapped in some kind of gray fabric, it trembled nearly imperceptibly, stench sprawling from it. Lauren's eyes fixated on the bundle. No. She couldn't investigate this time. Fighting the relentless tuggings of her urge to at least prod the quivering bundle, she backed away and swiveled out, inconspicuously placing the slate out of the bundle's sight.

She repositioned the bottom board, leaning it against the mobile home, then frantically wiped down her rabbit dress. Very little mud came off. Very far from clean.

The small porch was wasting already. The overhead panel had gone from white to green more quickly than Mr. Bevill had anticipated and was a source of embarrassment whenever the rare guest was allowed a visit.

The siding wasn't much better off. Though at one time it was red and white, it had surrendered to the sun long ago and had become a weathered pink and yellow-green.

Lauren squeezed her blue hands tightly.

The daunting screen door creaked. Mrs. Bevill welcomed her daughter as she stepped inside.

"Where the fuck have you been?"

"My... I looked—"

"You look awful," her mother jeered. Maybe it was the drink. A familiar strike reapplied Lauren's headache.

Mr. Bevill was within arm's reach before she saw him coming. A push sent the little girl to the floor. Her knee slammed into the rusty vent, leaving a waffled-shaped imprint.

It was too soon to cry. That needed careful timing. If it came at the right time, it had a decent chance of bringing the punishment to a quicker close. Too early meant she'd have to outdo that pinnacle of hysteria when the right moment actually came, not to mention the next time she was punished.

Beaded fabric and stray dirt and crumbs dug into her knees as she crawled the last few feet into her bedroom. She was only nine years old but getting conditioned. And anxiously awaiting acclimation.

As she gripped the sill, paint was forced under her fingernails. She looked out the window and tried to imagine. Something. Anything. Creatures she had drawn, animals she had seen. The tall man.

Mr. Bevill's disciplinary efforts moved him to grunt. It was almost time.

Almost.

It was too much to bear. She was less hardened than she thought.

"Daddy, I think I'm gonna die!" The desperate cry faded in and out with each strike.

He scoffed. "No you're not," he said, annoyed he'd had to expend energy to speak. His eyes were focused and his mouth wasn't quite a smile, but he certainly wasn't frowning. The inside edges of his eyebrows pushed toward his large nose.

Almost.

She gripped her legs. She hadn't meant to. The burn was too much to bear.

The sting across the back of her hands built upon itself like as though she were touching a hot stove, hurting more each moment after the initial touch.

There.

A loud grunt from him and a loud cry from her. He dropped the belt with a clink and pushed her to her bed.

Mrs. Bevill met him at the bedroom door, and

they left together. She sighed her irritation. "She's gonna have to wear leggings for a while."

The door shut.

Lauren lay on the floor, gripping her raw hamstrings. The pain thrummed, growing slightly more intense with each pulsation. She cried until she felt tired then pulled herself to bed as slowly as she could manage.

Wallpaper, held by long poster tacks, peeled from the walls, which were adorned with portraits of small animals, like her favorite bear cub picture and the one of the well-fed woodchuck. The sagging posters were tested every half hour or so when heat pushed through the vents. They were damp from occasional leaks, which Mr. Bevill rarely attended to and which seemed to multiply each time he did. Lauren's blankets slid from side to side as she shivered, still in her play dress. Mud seeped into the white sheets around her. She dragged her knees closer to her chest and listened to the TV blaring loudly in the living room. Mattress springs poked her side, but they were familiar. An almost pleasant bleakness.

She knew she was a little too young to accurately grasp what death was. Maybe she knew too little to do the concept of a genuine ending justice. But it had to be just a bit gentler.

Skirls emphasized her window's frailty, its incapacity to guard the girl from the one thing she wanted, the one thing that could pull her mind away from her burning legs. A loud, quick creak. She froze, holding the window midway up. The screen clicked as it hit the snow below.

The flakes looked broad and heavy, like the ash that had escaped the sides of the bag when her father had cleaned the fireplace at the old house.

She crawled through the window and jumped. The biting wind added to her incentive to dive under the mobile home.

Her moonlight lamp pierced through the slats surrounding most of its base. The bundle was gone, but the slate was still there.

The snow bit her knees.

She grabbed the slate and quietly crawled out from under the house, her eyes never leaving where the bundle had been. Where it *should* have been. She didn't feel solace in its absence. It was something she would have expected comfort from; she should have been happy the unusual and scary thing was missing. But the naked space under the spider-web-littered belly of the house only reinforced Lauren's feelings of remoteness and unrest.

The impression still left from where the bundle had sat was a garnish too unsettling for her to handle.

A rack holding a coiled hose became her step stool. She boosted herself up and into her room. The bleeding from the slate had stopped. The sludge that had dripped into the nearby creek now spared the bedroom of its putridity.

Her hands still had some blood on them. She wiped them on the slate's surface. But her blood didn't run off its face. Instead it pooled and settled into the shale-like layers. Although the edges of the slate looked brittle, its body was heavy and strong.

In the corner of the room, a desk stood next to a tall electric heater that hadn't worked for three blizzardous winters. Crayon markings decorated it in a disorderly abstract. Lauren headed to the desk and grabbed a pencil.

Cold air poured in through the window. Her goose bumps and clicking jaw pled for the muddy blanket. But she ignored them. Ignored everything but the slate.

She knelt and raked the pencil over it, delicately at first. Then deliberately.

She began with a head. Roark's? Sure, she could mimic his well by now. But a monkey's body? And a stubby tail? She giggled at the possibilities. Leopard gecko eyes, like those in the nature movie she had watched a dozen times. Long fingers and bat ears.

Her hybrid was complete.

His eyes bulged slightly, his jaw sitting in an underbite. A rugged and upright posture, all the more commanding of attention—even on her rock canvas. His shoulders were wide and pointed, his claws long and sharp. Claws? Had she drawn claws?

Had she drawn pointed shoulders, for that matter? She squinted. Something was wrong; the details were too exquisite. Distinct individual hairs topped his head and hung from his wrinkled chin.

She had never been able to develop such unique, shiny scales as the ones that armored his body. Her chuckle had trickled by the time a shallow clunk reverberated.

A bead of sweat dripped from her forehead, running dirt into her eyes. Another fell to the slate, which was free from her grip and staring up at her. She stiffened.

Roark twitched.

No. She was dizzy from the cold. She had hit her head too.

The drawing shifted again then lifted in pieces like shattered glass. In segments, the creature moved from the slate into the bedroom's damp air before the slices pulled into a single form again. Now the creature stood tall above the shaking girl.

Inky, absurd, and worst of all alive.

The wind outside stopped. The animals stopped. The weather and the beasts began to despise the girl in unison, angry that she had introduced something egregious.

Green eyes widened to the nightmarish creature. They shut, leaving a sliver of moonlight to crawl up the creature's body and illuminate his scaly skin. He stretched out his hand and sharp claws, his breath echoing in his throat.

What Lauren saw looked very different from her Roark. And the monkey-like frame and the unique eyes were bad ideas that looked worse when brought to life.

He bent his body slowly, sniffing as he moved toward her. His lined eyes locked on hers. Then on a scar on her arm, a scrape on her head. And finally he discovered the dried blood coiled around her legs. His concentration was broken, as was the silence, by a whimper.

"Roarkie?"

The creature jolted a scuffled step backward and tilted his head.

The TV shut off.

Lauren inhaled reflexively. The routineness of the curses and loud stomps that bellowed toward her room seemed foreign with the addition of her upright animation.

A sharp whirr. A pulse of wind. The poster, hangers, and papers scattered.

She was alone again.

Snapped from her shock, she tossed the slate out the window. Rushing to hide the evidence provided more warmth than her frustratingly holed afghan ever had.

By the time she had crammed the scattered papers under her bed and slammed her toys into her toy box, she was able to add sweat to her long list of discomforts.

Her sweeping foot sent the pencil flying underneath the bed. She quickly slipped under the covers just before hearing the familiar clunk of the doorstop pushing into a hole in the sheetrock.

The scowl that slightly wrinkled her mother's face didn't take away from her beauty; it only helped emphasize the differences between light and dark. Like the way her blue eyes contrasted with her straight black hair and thick dark eyebrows.

"Not another sound." The threat and tone behind the mandate had been tested before.

Worse than the muscle spasms from squeezing her arms to her chest was the aching tightness in Lauren's throat. She wouldn't have been surprised either way: if she was hit or if she was left alone.

The door slammed shut.

Mr. Bevill stood in the living-room-to-kitchen

connection. Not a hallway or useful space, just a transition to collect junk, or in the case of the Warner Sallman painting, dust.

The frame was cracked, the image far from an original piece. So it must have been sentiment, perhaps even superstition, that had persuaded the Bevills to bring it from house to house. Perhaps laziness, as surely was the reason a broken picture of a red-shawled man still hung opposite the Jesus painting.

Benedict XV stared at Jesus. The small rooms meant the pictures hung in close proximity to one another. Mr. Bevill wondered if Jesus wanted some solidarity from time to time.

A large mug bearing the boast "World's Best Bishop" crashed into Christ, settling the territorial dispute.

"You're fucking spying on me now?" Mrs. Bevill said from the living room. "Oh, don't even. I saw a shadow outside the window, and I—"

Her husband's eyebrows curled the way they did when he thought someone was joking—or when they should have been. His nostrils indented slightly, the way they did before a sarcastic chuckle. The way she hated.

Without much consideration for breath, she continued. "What do you think I was do—you can't even see—If I wanted to, I could have a line—"

The first ring stopped Mrs. Bevill's prating. The second lured Mr. Bevill's eyes to the counter, where his smartphone lay silent beside an unopened bottle of Quinta do Vesuvio and a small tapered glass. The third made him shove his hand into his left pocket.

He retrieved a flip phone and opened it. The irascible breath that pushed through the receiver pulled his shoulder blades together, pinning him upright.

The door swung and banged twice before closing. A chill hit his face immediately.

Without being aware of it, he walked toward the lake, failing to observe any foreign entity that polluted his haven. The voice in his ear had his total attention.

The slate lay cold and still, opposite a petrified Mr. Bevill. Minatory winds dusted its surface with large snowflakes, teasing an impossible disguise.

Claws pulled it into a delicate grip.

It had been nearly five years since they had been uprooted. Five years, and she'd grown tired of it. The anecdata of how things would change and soon. This impatience expressed itself most notably when her affairs became more regular. She was put off by the fact that he had been pulled out of the situation to begin with. She didn't need to know the details, didn't need to know *why* scrutiny was to be avoided in the first place. Nor why they needed extrication at all.

Regardless of the incentives, it had made him small. Less of a man. Her regret for their deliverance wasn't explicitly mentioned once, but the emotion was never missed by Mr. Bevill.

Part of her thought they would've been better off sticking it out, trying to make it on their own. Sure, she was in the dark to what the danger was or how bad it had gotten. But no one else had to leave, not so far as she was aware.

Or as far as she was dismissed in the rare moments she found the courage to tease a question.

A bigger part of her wished she had left her husband long ago. But the foremost part wanted an exciting, lavish life and the experiences and people that came along with the risks.

Before it all fell apart, she had met dozens of his coworkers, many of whom possessed evident fervor. She'd become very helpful, assisting with activities from cooking to cleaning, organizing music, and watching children. Always well positioned to catch admiration.

She didn't know what the conversation was about, but she felt fear through her anger. She knew very little about the black flip phone. But she knew she had seen one similar to it being given to him the day they were told it would be best to leave indefinitely. She also knew he had been instructed to replace it randomly, which kept her up more nights than she could count.

And she knew her handsome friend would be back the following day. So fuck it. Bottle in hand, she went to the bedroom.

Mr. Bevill closed the phone and stuffed it into his pants pocket. The lid pinched his calluses as he squeezed it between his fingers. He glanced at the gleaming lake and imagined drowning.

TWO

MALL FINGERS PARTED THE branches of a large spruce, snow misting from its lower branches.

Moonlight broke through a shadowy den. Through skinny, misplaced trees it highlighted the scars and bruises painted on a short, hairless arm. A young boy.

The woods seemed to crash on him in spinning waves, the tide of the floor jeering him with whirls. Violence of branches and blurs. Faint and light-headed, he felt as though he were being cast from the giant camouflaging tree. He gripped a needled branch with his left hand and clawed for balance.

Snow and moonlight spiraled together, competing to press through the spaces between the trees and rest on risen patches of ground outside their reach.

A symphony of low grumbles came, their propulsion guarded. The monotonous, muffled groans pounded on the wall of encircling evergreens, naked of animals.

But the boy's headache seemed to quiet the grim orchestra. Even his footsteps were muted by the throbbing in his head.

All the while, the trees made it worse, towering above and spinning him.

His feet dragged. One after the other.

The bottoms of his uncovered feet were numb. If he paused, the numbness would scale his leg. So he stepped. One by one, his trudges forced frozen needles into his purple skin. Snow jammed into the spaces between his toes as he raked one foot after the other with defiant determination.

Until he reached a smooth bump.

His foot stopped, resting against a leg and a folded arm tattooed with spots and bruises.

A tattered gray dress fell across a silken knee and over his foot. Sewn rabbit ears drooped from near her shoulders. Blood dripped from a thick knot in her tangled hair, down her head, and onto her lap. She was a dirty yet resplendent little girl. Sitting cross-legged. An angel washed in mud and snow.

Trapped. Quivering.

He felt it. Her fear. Her inability to look at him.

A petrifying sort of panic that narrated his oldest memories.

The revisited anguish. His fingertips were riddled with it, trembling inches from her shoulder.

A faint hint of the pinching grip on his own shoulder. His breath knocked from his chest with the memory. The trees bowed; he could feel them, just as he could feel the impact of the car door against his elbow. Shooting pain. The familiar, stern voice that pierced his ears. A scant lean. A curious frown.

He clenched his jaw, biting at the authority of the chemicals circulating through his body. A collection of enemies, powerful and familiar. And he was just a gaunt, weak boy.

No, he was courageous.

It was courage that had combated the men's advances despite the sprain they had dealt to his wrist. When he was apprehended, he'd had enough courage not to cry—not even when the plastic zip ties dug into his wrists with each bump the noisy car delivered.

Sure, he had cried when they'd caressed him, struck him.

But it wasn't the pain. It was the humiliation. The powerlessness.

"The world," they'd said, "is a putrid cesspool of a place." But they were the safeguards, ushers to the kingdom to those who'd been chosen. It was trickery too heavy to withstand. But, perhaps only for moments at a time, he had resisted. He was resilient. He could stomach it. And so far he'd outlived it. At times he wished he hadn't, wished he'd been killed.

But he wasn't.

For all the distress they delivered—to him and to so many angels like the girl in the rabbit dress—despite the anguish, he was alive. He'd outlived the redeeming, prayerful lashings; the coercive groping and worse.

And he could outlive the chemicals.

So he fought them. Squinted his eyes. Shook his head. And was allowed a brief pause in the replay, the dreadful flashbacks. Just enough to see it.

A slate in her right hand, reposed on her lap.

Her left hand had something in it too. She moved it slowly to the slate. Scraped it then paused.

The boy stood a little straighter. He would have jolted if his momentary paralysis allowed it.

Another scrape. Another pause. Expedited with each stroke.

A pounding in her chest. Plangent enough for the boy to hear, for the trees to hear. Scared and cold, he detected their scowls and silently pleaded for the girl to stop. His stomach turned with the sounds of the scrapes, and the escalated cadence emphasized his dizziness. The girl seemed to move back and forth like a muddy wave, his efforts to focus worsening his nausea.

He was still, aside from his right arm. It rose and delicately touched his side. Although he didn't look down, he felt the blood that seeped from the wound. A rare warmth.

"I'm Aiyden."

She stopped.

He didn't mean to speak. The words were extracted with a retch. In a muffled way, he could hear his own introduction, like someone had covered his ears.

The girl's attention didn't leave the slate. He was sure if he could see her face, he wouldn't see a blink.

His left hand crept into his pocket, pulled loose by its fibers.

"I threw them up sometimes."

His anxiety was agitated more by the renegade tongue that had nearly abandoned him than the looming giant trees surrounding him. He wanted to scream. Not from pain or even fear. But just to be able to scream. His lungs' recalcitrance with each fruitless attempt was more terrifying than the last.

"I couldn't every time." He felt regret; he hadn't tried hard enough to avoid each dose that had been forced upon him.

He also felt guilty. More than once he was happy to take them. If he knew they were coming to visit him, he yearned for a pill, a needle. He felt elation when the pellets of mercy were dropped onto his tongue. He happily swallowed and dove into crashing waves of numbness, denial, and obscurity.

Had he resisted—

Maybe he could have fought them. Sure, he would have been physically worse off for it, but what if he could have hurt one of them? What if he could have freed the other innocents who had shared his cold prison? And what about now? Could he be clear minded enough to save the angel at his feet, frightened and cold?

Green eyes followed a tear from his face to a powder, plastic, and pill combination resting in his palm. Crushed medication mixed with the sweat in his hands had created an odd color. He dropped the mixture to the ground and wiped his hand on his leg.

Her eyes went to the hand that gripped his side before they were piloted back to the slate; she looked almost ashamed that she had peered up at him.

There was a gap when she turned. A space just big enough for him to catch what her muddy hands had been scratching.

A bird? No…a dragon. Maybe not, but something

like it. Some blend that didn't belong together. Aiyden's eyebrows rose. Incredible abilities on such
a canvas. Realistic enough for him to hate it. Most
prominently reminiscent of a bat, yet it had scales
and spikes on its head and neck, with legs longer
than the rest of its body.

The loud pulls of Aiyden's sluggish saliva competed with the volume of the scrapes, the last one
a deep click.

The trees untwisted, stood straight at the sight
of the glacial unraveling of their sinister milieu. Icy
flakes disbanded from their clusters.

In fragments the sketch rose just above the
slate's surface, remaining flat. In the blink of an
eye, it broke into a dozen pieces and shot into the
air. About a foot above Aiyden's eye level, the pieces hesitated.

Accumulated snow burst from the clearing. The
shards of the drawing spun in a twisted miscellany
of snow, bits of branches, and dirt.

Immaculate.

In the dissipation of the snowy tornado, the
drawn beast hunched over. Claws protruded from
the tips of its wings—more like flaps sprinkled
with grisly gashes and red-stained tears—and
bored into the ground.

The creature's shoulders and back were its dis-
play of brawn. Agile muscle, different from the rest

of its spindly frame.

Aiyden released his side. He paid no more attention to his wound than the snowflakes that once again began to fall, sporadically prying through the trees and nestling onto his feverish forehead.

A sharp, upturned nose lifted. The beast's body stood in a terrifying shift, not fully upright.

The creature flinched spasmodically, its ears turning forward and back and forward again. Its eyes were focused. On the girl. On the boy.

She propped up on her elbow, and the creature turned to her. Each step pulled its thin muscles, veins wrapped tightly around them. Its head bobbed slightly from side to side; clearly it was poised to dash if warranted.

But it didn't jump, didn't advance.

The creature's eyes fixed behind them, as if it had forgotten the pair.

They weren't alone.

The bat thing wanted no part of it. Long, winged arms and legs pressed into the snow. There wasn't room enough to lift off and fly, assuming the torn wings had the capability, so the creature stumbled and scurried into the woods. All four limbs propelled it deeper into the darkness.

The pair. Left alone with the residual quiet. The girl in the gray rabbit dress stared at the slate, and Aiyden at the girl. He felt annoyed at his scatterbrained thinking, at his lack of formed thoughts.

But one formed well: a creature sufficiently vile to restrain the woods, a bat of some sort of magic, had fled due to its own dread.

"Come on," he whispered. Begged.

Sweat trailed from the edge of his hairline and tickled his forehead. His gut made its familiar turn. The acid from his stomach crept up his throat, escorted by his anxiety.

His hand moved. Slowly.

The girl sat straighter, her eyes not leaving the stone.

The chill of someone staring at him, standing behind him bit his spine, his neck—

"You can bring it if you want,'" he whispered.

Her cheeks bunched in an inauthentic, nevertheless grateful smile.

"Hold on to it, okay?" he said.

Her hand gradually held his; the other, the slate.

He didn't look away when he spoke, didn't shift. He coaxed with gentle hands and held her little body to his. A ripple of shocks coursed through the side of his neglected abdomen.

An hour. It had to have been. Muscle burned hot enough to hail his memory, to imply his shoulders would feel it again: the familiar grasp, the dominant grip.

The pain outmatched the fear. If he could scream, this time it would have been from anguish.

The girl didn't seem to mind the way her rescuer's wounds smeared red on her dress as he carried her away. Not enough to demand release. In fact, she'd stopped moving altogether. No fidget for comfort. No wriggle for security. Limp, aside from her clenched hands and the unintentional grasp that squeezed the slate into Aiyden's back.

To Aiyden, her emerald eyes weren't an inviting green. They were a foreboding shade, a warning of sorts. He caught just a glimpse, but too much. He wished he hadn't looked into them as he ran. Wide, dripping with tears. Worst of all, focused behind him.

Her face was scrunched as she buried all but her eyes behind his shoulder.

The panic in them told him to run.

He pressed her face softly into the space between his shoulder and neck then winced with the first step.

Now he heard it. Past his throbbing headache, past his spinning tunnel vision.

He heard its gawkish shifts and low, hungry grumbles. Louder. Louder. Whatever chased them was closing the gap.

Aiyden's efforts held less effect than he'd thought.

The monstrous galumphs drew closer and closer.

He wanted to be carried. More than anything perhaps, he wanted to be carried. Held, brought far away.

As he twisted through the woods and shrubbery, he felt the machination. The sabotage and betrayal, the disturbing blur of the forest. His pounding heartbeat. His short, loud breaths. Too many culprits to track.

Running wasn't entirely a consequence of the angst of being chased or the deliverance of the little girl. It was about escaping. Just this once perhaps and likely only for a moment. He could escape. Until the next captor took custody of him. A short win but one he desperately needed. A frail light to console him and a blockade to submission. A way to regain control.

Yes, even he could have control, despite the synthetic sway that coursed through his veins, the paralysis that toyed with his body. Even he could have control in the midst of his incomprehensible nightmares.

The intention, however, was relatively moot. In the half second he registered an insufficient relief of anxiety, he was wrenched downward.

The girl cried out. Not as loud as someone should, Aiyden thought, or normally would after the snap he'd heard. Her arm dangled from its middle. He loosened his foot from a coiled root and hoisted her to his lap. She resisted. The fucking slate. He wasn't reaching for it.

Besides, he was glad to be free of its weight.

Glad it couldn't hinder as he heaved the girl and shoved his heels into the frozen ground below him. The scuffs of his footsteps rattled in his head and aggravated him with the sluggishness of their rhythm. But it was only his he heard.

When he glanced back, his knees locked and his arms stiffened.

It seemed they'd put some distance between them and what had chased them. But there was no comfort with the realization.

Aiyden glimpsed the wounds on his feet, purple and black, bruised and frozen. The ground beneath them was biting and ruthless.

He traced his footprints with his eyes, leading from where the girl had dropped the slate. And saw it disturbed, giant hands grasping its sides.

He was at the whim of his eyes. He prayed for them to close, not to examine whoever had lifted the slate. He begged them not to scan—

But it was too late.

Long, dark garments. Torn enough to reveal traces of abraded flesh. Flesh darker than the filth that draped his body. Ebony stains on a mouthless mask. Only one thing beckoned his glare from the battered children. He caressed the slate's cracked brim, stared at his treasure.

Gentle fingers slid over Lauren's mouth. Her groan subsided as her rescuer kicked his feet backward along the biting snow. Her sleeves tenderly padded his bruised arms.

Push.

One foot at a time, he retreated until he felt the scratch of overhead branches, the rough bark as they passed a trunk. He had to stop, even if the masked thing hadn't let up as he had. Even as he withdrew into the shadows, giving up a chase he would have won. There was no neglecting the girl's injury anymore. No ignoring its severity.

Her knees folded to her stomach, her damaged arm clenched by the other, her head buried into her chest.

She wouldn't make it. Not without help.

Her eyes caught the blood seeping through his pajama-like clothes and onto his hand.

And through her folded arms, she saw him leave.

Morning came with curses and crying.

"Lauren?"

Mrs. Bevill's head throbbed with the early call. A narrow door slid open with a slam, aggravating her hangover.

"You need to get out here."

Mr. Bevill led his glowering wife to their daughter's room.

The walls were stripped of the wallpaper and posters. Mud and leaves lined the floor and were strewn on the small bed in the corner.

Mrs. Bevill's attention was drawn to the spot of blood that dripped down the side of the bed, a small russet stain at its base.

The restrained pandemonium inside the Bevill residence was lively enough to startle last night's cantaloupe from the grasp of a dark-faced woodchuck. A slammed door sent him back to the woods with only the briefest pause to retrieve the carelessly cast compost.

"This is my fault?"

"Jesus Christ." The distance between Mr. Bevill's paces increased with each rotation.

"So we're canceling with the Shumways then?"

"Thinking about it," he offered sarcastically.

"I'm calling the police."

"No." It was forceful but toneless. Yet all she heard was condescension.

"No? People are gonna—"

His head tilted in frustration; it would never be understood.

"We've talked about this."

"But she's never run away before!"

Maybe she was right. Not about calling the cops, of course. But maybe this was owed more alarm than he had assigned it.

"Look. I'll find her. We'll be right back. Watch."

Outside, Mr. Bevill shut the front door and missed his footing. A tumble down the concrete steps normally would have roused a curse. But everything was too quiet. The yard too still.

"Lauren?" It was a half-hearted call. Maybe just to break the silence.

The trees held the morning fog a bit longer than the cleared plot the mobile home sat on.

No way she would have gone inside the woods.

His beloved wasn't going to help him. Probably drinking already anyway. And so it was just him, which he usually preferred.

But not today.

Not when he spotted a heap near the edge of the lake, the tall weeds signaling its position with waves.

He closed his eyes, begging the universe, pleading he had conjured up the scene.

He heard each of his steps. He hated that.

But he took his time, giving every chance he could for the situation to change.

With each step, increasingly more sludge ridden than the previous, his knees buckled. It fucking couldn't be.

A girl.

His hand was suspended beside his face, an attempt to slap himself out of his daydream. But before he made contact—

Broken rope hung from each hand and foot, tangled into the thick weeds. Threadbare clothing ineffectually draped over her small frame.

It was real. Dreadfully real.

But her skin wasn't as tight as it should have been, he thought. A sponge to the murky water, until merely a sloughed layer remained, littered with lesions.

Tugged by a twisted ankle, the soaked body lay slumped on the bank.

A hurried pattern of slaps against the icy ground. Footsteps closed in.

"*Lau*—"

Mr. Bevill pulled his wife away before she could get close. His words were rushed and pushed together but more comforting than demanding. Like steering a child's eyes away from a dead pet.

"It isn't Lauren. Listen to me; it isn't her. I don't know who it is. Listen. Look at me. It isn't her."

Mrs. Bevill stared into his terrified eyes.

"Okay? It isn't Lauren." He led her away, restraining her attempts to move past him.

"Who—"

"I'm gonna figure it out and take care of it."

"I'm calling the cops."

"Listen."

Now he was demanding. Not like trying to steer a child's eyes. Like the child wanted to call the cops. And he had fucking said not to.

A burst of breath. Almost a chuckle. "Our daughter's missing. There's a body. And still?" She managed her hysteria less impressively than she thought. Sweat pulled from her forehead despite the cold weather. She shook.

He raised a finger and held his breath. "Don't fuck with me on this."

She was angry. Felt controlled. Frustrated. Terrified.

Whatever she was enduring, she walked back to their mobile home. No shades were opened. That was good enough for him.

Like a discarded doll, the dead girl's body scraped across a patch of thistle, her head bounced off a moss-ridden rock.

Mr. Bevill caught his breath. He double-checked the closed curtains then triple-checked.

His phone found itself in his palm once again. But with a second, hurried deliberation he didn't open it. He packed it deeper into his pocket.

He stooped and grasped the legs in front of him. The texture made him want to vomit.

Don't need to see this next part.

Feeling would be ghastly enough. Once he had a proper grip on the rings of broken skin coiled around her ankles, he closed his eyes and heaved. But his imagination focused on an image of her sludgy skin wiping off and sticking to his back. His eyes twitched open.

The woods scowled, and he ran into them.

He concentrated on the weight on his back, less attentive to his footing than he knew he should have been. Branches and stumps waited, poised to tug him and his burden to the ground.

But he was lucky.

A large, unfinished house sat before him; the walls were the holdup now. That's what he'd tell his wife. "Oh wait till it's finished! It's going to be a dream." It had to be. Her relocation and accommodating silence were hinged on the pledge of its fanciful qualities. Although the land was less than overwhelming, she'd say. The green of the trees wasn't her beach plan. Much more was needed before she'd have the paradise she'd been promised. The paradise, she'd think, that she was entitled—

Decayed flesh slumped to a crumpled heap.

Hardwood, a barrier to the elements and the unwelcome, had been broken. Shards of the plied veneer sat in the basement window frame, draped in bronzing cherry.

Mr. Bevill looked back to the discarded corpse and her tache noire stare. A few scrapes, some bleeding. But the blood on the boarded window was new. He knelt and dragged the body.

The lake might have cleaned the blood, but the scrapes would still be there. The sharpness and strength of the board suggested a decent gash. But nothing.

His stomps cleared lingering insects from the floor in the broken shed a few hundred feet from the construction project. Some of the snow caught on the gunk-caked mat, but mostly it hung to his deep-ridged boots.

If tossing metal containers of uncategorized screws against a splintering wall or kicking hardened bags of plaster of Paris with steel-toe boots is helpful in a search, it was no wonder he left only minutes later, shovel in hand.

He slammed the resistant shed door, registering his authority.

Once again he dragged the girl. Her neck popped with force. A large branch snagged her lip and stabbed through her mouth. He yanked, and with a snap, it split her lip and sliced through her cheek, and he was free to drag her further.

He shouted.

There was a "fuck" for the physical strain, a "fuck" for the bloody mess, and a "fuck" for the beginnings of putrefaction.

The break in his tirade was thanks to an open patch of raised ground. He jammed the shovel into a smooth wave of snow and dirt. In bunches he cast the dirt aside and under the trees closest to him. He thrust it again. He dug. Again. Again.

Anger contended with fear. Dirt competed with the corpse's blood for prominence on his tan overcoat.

Mrs. Bevill didn't notice the blood when she met her husband on the steps of their home. Her eyes were red and teary, but she spoke calmly. "I know what you said. I called the police. If we didn't, and we don't find her, you know what people will say."

His face paled, mirroring the snow. He stepped backward.

A corner by the stairs. A corner that had given him trouble before. And a decent amount of pain. It pushed into his shin, but he couldn't feel its sharp edge. He didn't hear his wife's inquiries either.

As he stepped out into the cool air, his legs felt weak. A breeze pulled his jacket flaps. He closed his eyes. He couldn't hear her tirade, simply the wind. The trees, the birds.

He didn't dream much. Hadn't for a while, but

what a perfect opportunity. If he could open his eyes and be back… Back before—

Focus.

His boots crushed the snow, each stride kicking up a mixture of brown and white. He could hear his wife now. Fucking shrills.

His mind raced for any reason not to call. Any reason not to hold down the number 1. He brought the flip phone to his ear. Someone picked up.

He was quiet for a second.

"My wife called the cops. My daughter's missing, and my wife—look they said they're sending someone and— No, no, it gets worse…"

They didn't want to hear. Not over the phone. The call ended.

They'd be coming.

A police car pulled into the drive before Mrs. Bevill could be too concerned about her husband's sudden departure. She tried to ignore the creak of the driver's-side door opening, the screech and slam of it closing. The dated model of the vehicle. Signs they hadn't sent their most decorated detective.

Rookie or not, he was handsome.

Her diaphanous nightgown caught a breeze. And his attention.

"Ma'am." He nodded with concern.

A brief flicker of her hand called him in. It clutched a tissue, which she brought to her tear-less face. The tea warmed her hands, and cooling it gave her reason to purse her lips.

"How long's she been lost?" He was tender, his voice strong and raspy. She told him timid, broken details of their discovery of her absence and even less of the child herself. He caught a word here and there.

His eyes scanned the mourning mother. "She's lucky to have you. You're a warrior; I can tell." He spoke like a young man. Enamored and excited. Grand promises he was clueless how to keep. Moved as a young man moves too. Unassuming and ignorant to his audience and the ease with which the game could be played. "I'm going to find her, and I'll make sure you're all right until I do." He sat up straighter. The hero in his own story.

He rose to leave.

"You play?" He pointed to a keyboard against the wall, cluttered with music books free of creases.

"A little. Do you?" Mrs. Bevill moved her hair to one side of her face then back again. That's what they did in her shows. It usually worked for her.

"A little. I could give it a go, but it's been a while."

"Please do!" Her voice was a little higher than usual.

His fingers played something from memory. Hers combed through her hair daintily.

He stared at her hands with admiration, at her ring with insouciance. By the time Mrs. Bevill's half-hearted resistance stopped, the situation didn't feel outlandish anymore.

THREE

S HE TASTED THICK, METALLIC blood. Not the familiar flavor of her own.

The carcass.

Scraps of hog flesh were draped over her like a sweaty blanket. Coarse hair tickled her raw flesh. Putrid through frothy sniffles.

An audible chill climbed her spine.

It was a diabolical exhibit, not quite comparable to the underworld she'd become accustomed to. Yet violent enough to intrigue even the more weathered demons.

A grisly spectacle sufficient to terrify, could she have seen, had her eyes not been gouged and consumed. They were only sockets now, coated in blood and a totality of darkness that amplified her panic.

The slate was close by.

She could feel it. Smell it, beyond the rotting flesh that guarded her from the freezing air.

The aches climbed from her pulpified legs to her fractured skull.

She ran her left arm over her right leg, gently massaging a protruding bone covered in soft, warm liquid. Her spine was displaced and twisted beyond straightening. When she moved, it curved with her.

Her assailants had been thorough.

The ground wasn't coarse; in fact, it was soft. She lay still. As still as the neuralgia and sporadic spasms permitted. But she had little time to pause, little time to fantasize about death.

Footsteps approached. Not silent, not cautious.

She longed for the disguising darkness of her world. A pause to collect and plan.

In her blindness she couldn't know the state of the summoning grounds, the place where she had first called to the underworld. She couldn't be sure if the other witches had fled for good or if their jealous attempts to mimic her successful conjuring would begin again and bring them back to the infamous woodland.

Nor could she discern the state of the world she'd left long before.

But she understood what would befall her if she were taken in under earthly care. She needed more than they could provide. Somehow.

The footsteps.

They were too close.

She strained. Let out a nearly mute grunt. Past the lifted flaps of animal flesh, she felt it. Its rugged, sharp edges. Its stony, waved surface. Her stomach turned as though she were facing a thousand-meter plummet.

Almost more grisly than her mangled bones and cleaved flesh was a piercing high pitch. She remembered its unforgiving intrusiveness; she'd crossed the chaotic cosmos before.

She recalled the colors tainting the tunnels between worlds. Colors splintered into sandy particles. Purples pushed unseen into marred muscle. Blues teased the tenderness of her dislocated limbs.

And she felt suspended in the unkind air.

Passing distant lamentations as she was tossed about, she anticipated a sort of crash to the shadowed labyrinth. And all the while the piercing high pitch. Louder and louder and louder. Her stomach swirled; her muscles twitched.

Pushed by grainy winds, towed by dry water. The environmental mix climbed into her nostrils and mangled mouth, filling her lungs and strangling her throat.

The familiar atmosphere brought wailing harsher than the piercing tones, more disquieting than the asphyxiation. Somehow. Not moans for help, nor entirely expressions of distress. They were nause-ating, hopeless cries begging for death.

Dizziness ushered her the hope of her own death. A weightlessness in her brain that—

Her head crashed cruelly.

Her limbs plunged to a scalding floor, her arm shattering with the impact. Yet she remained as quiet as manageable (in such a world, silence was a rare ally to the sufferer).

She knew she wasn't in the veiling black; the slate wasn't where she'd left it. Her retreat through its earthly counterpart had been foiled. It had been moved.

The distance of the wailing was an oddity that accompanied the blistering of her back. Yes, she was much too far away from the tortured howls. And only one place could transform the roaring groans to a chorus, twisted upward and echoing like a continuous song. Whatever heart she main-tained sank, almost attempting to escape and greet the weeping.

Recollection of the structure—stone carved by the fingernails of the tormented, chiseled with bones pulled from living hosts, perched on a cliff—roused terror in her. And remembrance of the most baleful—The Ghoul, as often called in the many tongues of the afflicted and abused serenading his domain from below—inspired a panic. Hysteria communal with yielding. Acceptance despite the tumult.

She had a face ironed to her memory to go with the reputation. A clear image despite her blindness. A claim of recognition not many could make.

Steps scuffled within the structure and toward her amid the harrowing echoes. Whispers drew slowly and between wheezing breaths.

He breathed deeply through his nose—which was damaged, judging by its broken, snore-like sound—and choked back phlegm.

It was dread, to be certain, that beckoned The Witch's focus. But intrigue, bewilderment perhaps, that sabotaged her attention to the scraping, dramatic limps. Queries whirled through her mind. Those of the past, those of a volatile future, a suspicious present—

How could she have forgotten? For all her wondering, she'd neglected the most likely subject of the inquisition. Surely the only reason she was still alive.

The unrecalled might have been lost if not for a protracted, shrill hiss and simply a name.

"Rei."

The name was escorted on velvety air. Smooth and cooling, it coated her bloodstained face. A haze from his fingertips kissed her forehead, and an impossible process of repair began. The substance cradled the sockets of her eyes and filled the emptiness in them.

She saw him.

Had she never encountered The Ghoul before, his demeanor would have fooled her. Feeble, crouched, decrepit. A woeful, ashy demon.

But a master of demons.

He held the slate in his sable claws and tilted toward her.

The gray vapor that had swathed her eyes and given her second sight—whether blessing or curse—quavered down her arms. Draped her back. Overlaid her defiled body in its entirety. Her spine straightened with impossible torment.

In the dislocation's undoing, she heard him again.

"A reckoning is coming for those who've opposed me." His prophecy held no threat. A vow glided on the restoring vapor. "But I offer you a forgiveness of debt."

He stooped next to where she lay. His rage was apparent in the flare of his yellow eyes, but the tail of his proclamation clutched an inflection of urgency. An eagerness propped on an invitation.

"Mend the portal. Lift the treasonous barrier. Make it obedient to my will."

A bony fist clenched to his chest and pounded deliberately. He stopped. The next charge was whispered. Delicately delivered.

"And bring him to me. Bring me the abomination you pried from its surface. Bring me Rei, Witch."

He was still more than a bit hunched. And the tiny pupils of his bright eyes seared her own. His dark skin hid a wealth of scars.

He shuffled backward, allowing her a coun-terfeit gap, granting her little time to process before continuing. "Unbreak the link your sorcerers desecrated. Resume the entwining of our worlds— progress which your companions interrupted, sabotaged…"

He wouldn't win her over with enthusiasm for his own agenda.

No, she must be coaxed if Rei was to be prompt-ly before him—if he was to be capable of returning to earth.

"But what do I truly offer?" The Ghoul contin-ued. "The strength to issue your own retributions. To those who are your constant oppression."

He had her attention.

"Power that would dwarf the united talent of the soft-hearted necromancers and the sorcerers who tried to inhibit. On their earth you were envied and worse—despised and hunted as a witch. Superior-ity you should have been worshiped for. Here, dealt with as waste."

She scanned her freshest wounds.

"They were only supposed to restrain you," he said. "And bring you to me."

He wasn't tender with his gaze, a presumably unfeasible feat, but he seemed to harbor a little less rancor than usual. And his grip on her splintered arm was...tame?

The vapor felt thicker still. She detected its tug on her forearms. Her grip clutched the smoky dissipation.

"Power for consequences," he encouraged.

Power she could feel in her hardened shins, the relaxing of her back. Power to see with unshackled clarity. And she could have stood again, she knew, if not for fear.

"Take it," The Ghoul coaxed in a stern whisper. He stretched Earth's companion passageway toward her.

She wanted to investigate the sincerity in his eyes, but she knew better than to delay, to pause until she knew why he offered it, why he offered a second chance. She held out her hands and gently pinched the slate by its rough sides.

"Bring him," he finished with an exhale and a wheeze.

His lingering hiss stung her ears.

The vapor. It hadn't just swaddled her wounds; it flowed into her. In the incandescence, the strange beauty of her repaired, grayish skin, she was distracted. And The Ghoul's departure was unde-tected—that is, until his moist steps drifted from an adjoining room.

The Witch stood and followed.

She peeked inside a dark, stench-ridden cham-ber coated in violet and ruby. Veins slithered from the ceiling, down the walls, and converged to mul-tiple, floor-born sacs (more empty than occupied). Inside the sacs, small creatures squealed for free-dom, their efforts to pierce the ductile exteriors as tiring as they were futile.

The Ghoul grunted, sniffing the larger sacs that had collapsed from their weight. The most sizeable he sniffed with particular attention and forced a small tear on its tip with a pinch. Filthy black liq-uid drained from the hole to his outstretched hand then to the floor.

He left the discharging sac for the smallest: an empty, distinctly veiny and gossamer pouch.

Tiny, fleshy fingers perforated through the larg-er sac and frisked the hole. Stretched and tore it wider.

Now The Witch had a choice, or few, regarding where to concentrate her wonder. To observe The Ghoul or witness the progress the stubby fingers made. Or perhaps to focus on her strange embodi-ment of the vapor, the sinewing engulfment of her arms.

Her legs too shared a sturdy strength, a tightness like that which followed her recurrent sprints from affliction. But whichever focus would have been more prudent, her eyes impetuously shifted to the hole bored inches across.

A hideous, infant hellion spilled from the sac to the mucousy puddle below, sounding its tumble with a newborn cry. With the sac's moisture underneath its swollen limbs, the infant skirmished to roll, crawl, and drag itself along.

Once it was on its belly, its cries were muted in the anticipation of freedom. Freedom, if not for the clasp around its ankle and a jolt to the sultry air. The child hellion squealed like a hog pressed to a scalding tank, its frail body suspended.

The Witch paused in the doorway. A grim choice: a hall bearing rooms with foreign woe or the hole The Ghoul had clambered through in his departure from the structure.

"Bring him," his hiss demanded.

Had The Witch slowed and focused, she might have noticed the bodies along the walls of one of the cave-like rooms had quickly become more numerous. And less lifeless.

Suddenly the overlooked company was forcefully

announced as a naked demon accosted her.

A female.

An almost pleasant spectacle in such a world, though the naked female's eyes were mournful and her body shriveled. Her mouth was collapsed inward. A gash was open and infected down her forearm.

Gloom tumbled from more onlookers. Some examined the intruder. Others lay still, coiled on the floor.

The most physically fit were restrained, metal clasps filleting their necks. Those with deformities and other natural restrictors were left in breathing heaps here and there. Dried blood stained their thighs, smeared down their legs. They shuddered and whimpered at the newcomer.

Only the closest discerned The Witch's fear, picked up on the nonaggression in her bewilderment. She thrust herself forward, bound hands raised, a begging anxiety in her clouded eyes. She misjudged her intensity, knocking her final hope for liberation to the ground. The Witch flailed unsuccessfully for balance and fell too, body at the mercy of the hellish gravity.

Scrambles toward the fleeing witch. Swipes of panic, desperation for rescue. More and more joined the advance.

The Witch pulled herself to her knees and

scrambled toward the doorway, not sparing a second to stand. Only showing care not to drop the slate dangling in her hand.

When she could stand, she ran. Into a mottled maroon hall. This time to follow The Ghoul's path. And to climb through the hole that opened to the top of his crumbled castle.

Blood ran from the peak of the mountain, trickled and dried down its sides. A mephitic, polluted stage.

The screams of fear, the groans funneled a chorus upward.

Black at the base of the crag. A thick fog swallowed those who swarmed it, seeking the veiling darkness. In waves the haze swallowed silhouettes of demons. Through tunnels of doom they stamped-ed for asylum. Yelps from the molested and tortured trodding through an unending maze poured from within.

But they were silenced by something unseen before they reached The Ghoul's structure.

And for a moment, a memory perhaps wrought by the terror, The Witch felt the rips once again. The blows. Rei's stalwart stalk of the mob. The darkness from the excruciating, slow blinding. Dual blades of bone raised in Rei's rescuing hands before the blackness was complete.

No. She had to focus. She'd have her revenge.

She climbed down The Ghoul's crag, finally crouching into the colossal shadow that footed it. The decomposition of mangled corpses clogged her nose.

Her free hand swayed. Black fog ran through her fingers as she attempted to maneuver through it. It mocked her with disorientation. Congested her lungs. Strangled her throat. Only a few steps in, she couldn't breathe.

So she lay on her stomach, seeking a sham asylum: a foot-high space between the ground and fog. Littered corpses, thorns, blood.

An instant char afflicted her stomach and legs and hands. Bristles like daggers failed to pilfer the slate from her hand. Lacerations, but she didn't wail.

With distance from The Ghoul's mountain, the air thinned.

Faster and faster she crawled. She couldn't slow, couldn't stop. She had nearly found it.

Her fingers tapped on a small crack, and she traced along it. Almost there. It split wider and deeper into the darkness. She followed it on the ground, pulling herself along as quickly as she could. Screams of panic and desperation barreled toward her. Painful stomps of the fearful.

The Witch's hands flickered across the wounded ground as slowly as she effectively could. The crack was wide and oozed warm liquid.

The indention. With replacement of the slate, Rei's suspicion would lessen. Perhaps it would keep him from entertaining the idea of a repaired allegiance to The Ghoul.

So she lay the slate into the sunken space, letting it slide from her hands one side at a time.

Before the second hit the embers of the soil, her hand swiped gently over its face, and The Witch was gone.

For the evil that lurked there, for the caution it commanded, there was a lot of running in the woods.

When it was the cop's turn, he was less concerned with sound than those before him. The crunches beneath his hasty strides, for example. Raucous enough to scatter remote beetles and crickets from the eastern border of the woods.

His warrior mien could have been a bit of showmanship, but no one was there to judge. Besides, a tightly gripped AR-15 wasn't overkill; it was preparation. Provoked by shuffling leaves, he pointed it and grinned at his attentiveness.

The grin fell quickly.

Razor wire. A twenty-foot bed of it at the woods' edge, constructed at varying levels about a foot in height and inches in separation. Grass had grown over much of it, which somehow made it more obvious he should have heeded the warning. The command not to interfere. The command that didn't make any sense, that he had to disobey, was sprinkled with solemn sanity.

The gloom and weeds had hidden the impressive metal mattress, reinforcing the idea that his commanding officers weren't facetious with their warnings to stay at the station. To not get involved. Nor their threats as casual as he'd taken them.

He rotated, weapon at his hip.

Surely he wasn't lost already. The path was difficult to trace, difficult to track, though the charitable spruces prevented a stockpile of snow. Negligence perhaps? No. He was simply alert for the girl; that was it. Distracted in the totality of his concern. A fucking sacrificial professional.

The path became rubble, an effort clearly abandoned many years ago. But the scattered rubble led him to a rather new structure: the bare bones of a house.

He stopped.

Multiple locks were latched to large metal doors. The woods were gray-white. Even the evergreens didn't seem green. Not a real green anyway. The red bulkhead glared as though it were the only color in the woodland.

There was no sound either. No creatures scuffling about. No birds, no wind.

A concealing panel compelled him to investigate. He sent the butt of his rifle through the boarded window and looked in, squinting into the obscure basement. He knelt and leaned in closer. Something...something small. Like a child, terrified and shivering.

The smell hit his nose just before the lumpy side of a split stub of wood knocked him out and sent him to the ground.

Beautiful eyes. Droopy and blue. Unbothered to witness the crack, the spray of red over the sill and through the basement window. Big eyes on a short, shadowed frame watched the trickling trail of blood.

A shivering girl listened to the familiar scuffling steps. Alongside her jailer, an unconscious man in uniform grated across the icy ground.

There was a winding and wriggling of metal, and a punch at the bulkhead door. The doors didn't move. Another twist. A click. The left bulkhead door opened. A troubling, acute screech rung with tedious emphasis, as if shaving the matte lacquer of a blackboard with a fingernail.

Then a clink and a clunk. The alternating scrapes and cracks and thuds repeated. And again. At the conclusion of each rotation, a tooth or two capered down the steps and skid across the concrete floor. Blood trailed the procession.

Lethargy overburdened the girl's attempts to pry her eyes from the gore. And when the leak was plugged with a cloth, not so gently forced into the cop's draining mouth, vomit wriggled up her esophagus.

A circular LED light was tapped and turned on, illuminating the petrified expressions of several children.

But only one moved much worth noticing. She sheltered her eyes from the light as much as her reluctant arm would cooperate (only a bit more than the zombie-like teeters of the others restrained with her, like the child who'd witnessed the lawman's collapse).

She felt the limit of the rope coiled around her right leg. About fourteen years old, she wore a yellowish shirt and torn pants. Her twisted hand stretched past the confining leash and into her captor's sight.

Next to a few jars, ropes, and restraints, a bottle clanked on the third shelf of a rack. Much more prevalent were the littered needles, syringes, and glass vials of liquid. Needles gave the captor much more trouble than the pills. As such was the case, he enthusiastically, though reticently, welcomed those who would do the work for him. Still, those who showed resistance to the medication had to be given the extra measure of chain restraints. Yes, it meant having to hear complaints of how unacceptable the broken skin and markings of shackles were when he delivered the children to their buyers. But he couldn't risk any more breakouts.

A noisy metal cage, crafted crudely with an unfitting chain-link fence, slammed shut after he grabbed something off one of the shelves.

A large pill fell from his hand to the yellow-shirted girl's. She pulled her outstretched arm to her chest, crawled to a shadowed corner of the basement. He scoffed and shook his head. And she huddled with her prize as a metal chain was clasped around her ankle.

A stomp on the cop's spine. It gave the man holding the coil of rope confidence that he'd behave.

A gob of spit splashed the butchered jaw.

He tugged on his uncooperative overcoat and bent down to bind him.

The black sedan wasn't silent, but there was something clean about the way it whirred down the drive. The pop of gravel under its thin tires didn't agitate Mrs. Bevill as it usually did. Its lights dimmed before it came to a smooth stop.

Sporting charcoal suits and ebony ties, two men stepped out of the vehicle. Their frames were similar: broad and sturdy. Only a tint of stubble on their faces.

The introductions made their brief, uncomfortable circuit. Slight bends of their backs, tips of their heads. No names. Announcements that quickly corroded into a single demand: an audience with her husband.

Mrs. Bevill tried to guide them inside. They declined.

They stood by their vehicle, suspending further conversation. Until, as Hollywood would have it, Mr. Bevill sauntered out of the woods immediately following their decision to linger without drink or unctuous company.

"Police?" one said to him.

It would have been easy to miss the minute gesture made toward the Taurus. But Mr. Bevill was fixated. If one of the men would have sniffled, he would have given significance to it.

Mrs. Bevill was sent inside before a response was delivered. The door banged twice before closing.

"He's locked in the basement." He thumbed toward his project house.

A lamp flickered on. The stench larruped their nostrils. Their composure turned into outrage for the filthy state of the basement. The suited men covered their mouths and noses and coughed.

And their silence marked their fury.

Neither broke their professional demeanor, but one became slightly more animated after a pause.

He was the taller of the two. He seemed to have two teeth in the place of one, Mr. Bevill noticed. And the rest were less than straight.

"What's the best you have?" The lack of aggression in his voice terrified Mr. Bevill more than a shouted charge would have.

He stuttered and his eyes scanned indiscriminately. The double-toothed man put a hand on Mr. Bevill's shoulder and did a half wink as he spoke. Perhaps an attempt to humanize the situation. To calm the subordinate.

"Grab me the very best you've got." The near smile. The way he stressed "very best" sounded like he was encouraging a child to retrieve their favorite toys. It flipped Mr. Bevill's stomach and crammed chunks of a previous meal into his throat.

Eventually he selected two children, frantically examining them with jittered glances: a girl, the least squalid and most durable, and the only boy. But Mr. Bevill's anxiety didn't lift in the slightest. Nor was he relieved to see the men leave, dragging their zip-tied selections to the trunk of their black sedan.

They hurled the children onto the ground. Or something. Maybe the trunk. He couldn't discern thud from thump.

And he didn't waste the privacy he was granted. The side of his foot became a bulldozer that pushed along the feces and urine he had long since grown tired of cleaning up. Soon he was on his hands and knees near the cop, bleach in one hand a rag in the other, scrubbing an unbeatable mess.

Without breaking stride, the shorter of the men descended the bulkhead stairs and met the cop, revolver in hand. A .410 defense load painted heroic gray matter on Mr. Bevill's legs and feet and the portion of the concrete already smelling of the disinfectant.

Mr. Bevill fell backward and gasped, immediately regretting his inability to conceal his fear.

But could he be acquitted of the charge of once again risking exposing their operation now that the cop was dead? Or—and his heart sank at the likelihood—next in line for elimination?

"Right," the taller man said, not bothering to review his colleague's handiwork. "Gas?"

"I...I...have a lit—"

"Get what you've got here. The doors, the walls, the cop..." He indicated with casual, guiding fingers, as if this were an ordinary conversation.

Mr. Bevill thought of the cans around the corner, behind the chain-link cage. He shuddered at how little he had. At how incensed they'd become.

He turned. The floor came closer. Closer.

Sometime later Mr. Bevill woke alongside the brutalized lawman, tied and gagged. His own jaw was fractured.

Some terrible karmic mutilation. He didn't quite let the thought form. But he couldn't help giving the idea a voice, recalling the cop minutes before his slug-delivered decapitation.

A bitter taste festered in his mouth: half amber wingtip, half Bevill blood.

The idea of a cinematic restructuring of his affairs had piqued his interest before. But this was a less than satisfying denouement. And more than betrayal.

But he wasn't delirious with rage or fright, as he would have expected.

Perhaps it was his ignorance, but he felt bewildered. Like his life was little more than time passed. It couldn't be concluding.

Meaning was imminent. Surely.

He was going to retch, large droplets of gasoline running down his nose and mouth. But he didn't feel any panic to gasp for air. The facts rattled in his head without permit to rage.

The light flickered outside the door, and the flames crawled in like a slow wave. But he could only think about the meeting. Men sitting and talking about his peril as though it were their own. But they valued him. They kept saying that. They valued him.

They had been set up with chips and drinks. The plaque on a custom microsuede table had read, "Pot Limit Omaha." But the box of cards above it had lain unopened.

They'd stressed potential outcomes and explained there would be resounding aftereffects for any decision, but most troublesome with further exposure. And they valued him. So they brainstormed.

There were many specific details. Some that resonated at the time, like the sensation of ceremony as he surrendered his white collar upon request.

As he sat doused in gasoline, most details seemed too trivial to recall. But he remembered feeling they had come to a decision long before the meeting. A rehearsed plot if there ever was one.

He had waited and listened.

They decided.

A new home. The location selected, in large part, for the reputation that came with it. A reputation of loss, tragedy, woe.

No suspicion. No concern. And his indiscretions would be forgotten.

His work could start anew.

Mr. Bevill's claims of cynicism were repeatedly unraveled by each promise made to him and the way he eagerly placed confidence in them. How hastily he accepted the mandates affixed. Until he sat there, the last of the gasoline saved for him. Just enough to kill, not enough to make it quick.

He wasn't sure if the exhale was born from relief for an imminent finale or from depression. Or if the vomit that fell over his disassembled jaw had culminated from the beating itself or the gasoline—or if it was due to the skin peeling from the arm of the child nearest the bulkhead.

The flames had begun their push into the basement.

The screams rose from one child to the next in near perfect unison as the fire escalated.

The yellow in one girl's eyes matched her torn shirt. She sat trembling, chin wrinkled with a pout. Isolated to the core and aware of it.

She looked closely at the pills rolling around in her sweaty hands. Some new, some more or less a week old. She tried to fixate on them, but the heat of the flames demanded the attention of its participating audience. She tried not to listen, but the screams swelled and rose and clawed into her ears. The medication touched her lips, a kissing promise of liberation.

She closed her eyes and swallowed.

Aiyden's tromps agitated his wounds, drawing from the ground through his bare feet and up his legs, which were exhausted and underweight.

He had been stern about the command. She would wait. She had to. But how long?

His stomach turned and fell.

He recognized the ground, the rocks, the building not far ahead. His eyes caught the smoke escaping through the broken basement window and the cracks in the bulkhead.

He wished he were lost. Wished he'd stayed with the girl.

But it was the screams that made him run toward, rather than away from, the familiar horror; made him approach the broken window. He touched the tip of a shard of broken board lodged in the frame. Clasped his side where it had punctured. Bloodstains clung to the wood, and squeals blasted past him as he wiggled it free.

One girl was instantly visible through the ascending smoke. Stiff fingers tried to flick the flames off. She shook her arm hopelessly. Her mouth was wide but silent, aside from sporadic gasps for air through the choking smoke.

Aiyden jumped to the floor; the debilitating snap that followed incited a shout. It was loud but muted by the children who lined the basement's edges. Cries of pain, of terror.

But the bishop sat silently, tied and gagged on a claret liquid bed. A policeman lay next to him, his brains a hashed piccalilli. Both were temporarily safe from the expanding flames.

Aiyden's ankle rolled with his attempt to run, but with fear and wrath, he careened to a shelf. Pushed a pair of pliers aside. Swiped and knocked over bottles, tapes, and rope. And finally grasped a medium-length knife.

A small girl bound with thick, white, poly dacron rope sat nearest the flames. Abruptly wrenched from their reach, she cried out. With several strokes, he cut her free. Then the next. And the next.

He dragged one by one to a flameless corner of the basement.

"Wait here. Wai—"

His breathing strained, Aiyden turned to the numerous children who were still bound. He plodded painfully to the next one, the child in most imminent danger.

His heart sank.

Chains.

A crack shot up his knees as he fell in defeat.

His brain rattled his options with uncharitable chaos. He would have to hustle—but where would a key...no—to those he'd released. He had to get them out first. At least ensure complete liberation for a few.

So to the broken window he began to tug them, one by one.

"Come on!" he screamed, incoherent in his anguish.

He tried to coax, demand, plead assistance from their droopy bodies, but their movement was beyond their control.

His hamstrings were tight and tore. He clenched his jaw. Groaned as he hoisted them through the window, favoring the broken bits of him. Adrenaline teased sure footing, waiting to strike should he trust it.

In fact, he hadn't even checked to see what had broken. Perhaps his foot or shin. Whatever the ailment, it was a cruel play so on par that it slithered into his plight without recognition.

The flames roared. Excruciating howls seemed to bow the walls outward.

Blood and mud clogged chipped nails outside the basement. Feet kicked pointlessly from the narrow, broken window. The prisoners were sedated but desperate.

Tears deluged Aiyden's face. The fire slithered up the shackled children as he hobbled from the window. To the counter, the toolbox, the shelves. Drawers were opened and rattled off their hinges before crashing to the concrete. Bottles and boxes were cast aside.

"The key! I can't find the fucking key! Where did he fucking put the key?"

The children shook and bellowed in the ghastly frenzy.

Aiyden ran to the bishop. The gag, being caked in blood, vomit, and splintered teeth, demanded a hard yank for extraction. He was poised to demand a key, but as soon as the soaked rag hit the floor, the bishop mumbled intelligible pleas.

Groaning, Aiyden stood, dizzy from desolation and the relentless catastrophe. The basement ceiling, marinated in the roaring flames, seemed to be counting down the minutes until it surrendered to the heat. Despite the oft-promoted dropping and rolling, the children couldn't escape the flames. Shrieking, they tossed their bodies from side to side.

They tugged at their restraints. Skin peeled

from their bound legs as the metal became a brutal, erratic grater.

Aiyden howled an angry, defeated shout. He knelt to a shackled girl and wailed as he drove his knife into her ankle and back out. She howled and he brought the knife down again. And up. And down. Grunting. Stabbed and scraped and slashed.

Until all but detached, her foot drooped and swiveled, and darkness abducted her vision. Aiyden stood and stomped her ankle, snapping the bone and freeing her from the shackle.

With a heave, he lifted her body and hopped, towing his uncooperative foot toward the window. The boil in his spine impeccably matched the scald of the flames as he lifted her and pushed her through the window.

He turned. A shout of agony blared more clearly and audibly than any sound he had grumbled or moaned or sobbed in years.

Slurred speech from the next child corrected enough to allow her to cry a bone-curdling, one-word plea. And with an outstretched arm she begged.

"*No!*"

Aiyden grasped the ineffective arm and drove the knife into her ankle.

She screamed and vomited as he disconnected foot from body. He stood to carry her, but his spine at long last failed him. A spasm hurled them to the floor. Aiyden pulled the last of his strength from his remarkable reserves. One arm pulled the one-footed girl, the other pushed along the concrete until his shoulder brushed the far wall.

Adrenaline dissipated as a thought wafted into his consciousness: *All of it. For nothing.*

Red drained from his garments to unite with the gore below. The flames hissed and mocked his labor, engulfing the remaining chained children.

Thick tears slopped with mucus and blood and grime. A fetid blend that collected in his hands and tarnished his face. He cradled his head and roared as loud as he could. At the flames' passing bite. At their finalizing tyranny.

The bishop's awareness slowly returned to him. Hands assisting a hopping leg and hurt back. The head of a boy—a child he had restrained before—lowered to the thinner smoke.

Of course.

It was the child who had escaped, broken the window. It was he who had allowed another to escape: the girl he'd found by the lake.

Aiyden.

The lanky blond boy he'd stalked, a plain-view pursuit that had lasted weeks. The boy he'd attempted to counsel through the grief of a lost father.

In disobedience, he had intended Aiyden for

himself alone. Quite separate from the operation he oversaw.

Aiyden. The boy who resisted his attentiveness. Who took the solace of a bishop's office for granted, along with his nurturing intimacy.

But despite his infatuation with the boy, he reluctantly had added him, as ordered, to the number of children outside his reach, reserved for those above his station.

And with these remembrances, panic gripped his throat.

The bishop pushed against the basement's backmost wall and groaned a blood-filled petition as the boy staggered toward him.

Aiyden knelt on the bishop's stomach and plunged his head to the floor, forced the blade into his mouth. The boy's eyes were red with anger. An absolute, torrid anger. He drew the blade back and reveled in the episode of retches and chunky gargles and gasps for air that would not be collected. And thrust again. Over and over. His mouth. His eyes. Eventually only the floor.

His hand was speckled and ruby. It lifted to puncture the chest of the cruel cretin of the cloth.

The flames snatched the blade from Aiyden's hands, covering his body and killing with a vile, stinging kiss. They burst throughout the basement, through the window. Engulfed the hollow home.

Scarlet bodies, severed of feet. The liberated children lay unconscious outside the broken window.

And a fiery cocoon swallowed them in their sleep.

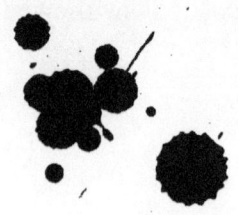

FOUR

LAUREN'S EYES WATERED.

The green in them was graying. The resulting color glowed like a crystal, till the man before her could see the defined imperfections of his mask in their reflection. The cracks and flaps. The layers that covered the wilting portions, and only just.

She hadn't heard him—a miscalculation she'd have attributed to his devilish paranormality in hindsight. And not to the chill that pulsed through her broken arm, crept through her purpled toes. The fever that seized her and disoriented her. The delirium that stretched her arm to the brute, unladen with caution.

Yes, her arm was extended. But she didn't mean to do it. It had moved on its own. It *had* to have moved on its own.

Yet it wasn't a lost battle to restrain her arm. She hadn't lost control because she didn't want control. Not entirely. If she had maintained authority, she would be culpable for its twitch toward the masked man's hand. It would have meant the consequences of taking the slate from his grasp would be hers alone.

Why did she have to break from the trance-like hysteria? When his nails scraped the slate's corner, her eyes followed them perfectly. The relic dangled in his hand, and amused, the masked Rei held it to the girl. It slid from his hand to hers without objection, her broken arm cradled to her body.

Now what?

He brandished a foul portion of flesh that drooped like an omen. A meal interrupted or about to begin. Averting her eyes from the butchered morsel only meant more consideration could be given to his appearance. A faded ebony cloak failed to veil him completely, but details were obscure beyond mismatched clothing and a giant frame.

An oddness to the ticking in her chest. Rapid flutters followed by long, pausing beats pulled her focus inward. Lauren's anxiety met her heart rate at the peaks and waited there for its return. Young. Naïve. But not stupid. Something was wrong, and without help, the problem would deteriorate quickly.

She meant to resist even a flinch, but gravity strained her slate-bearing arm till it touched her side.

Her fractured forearm throbbed.

With a pause that felt longer than minutes, she tried to calm her mind. Her anxiety lurched and demanded immersion in her plight. Big picture and meticulous. Down to the next single movement.

His mask nearly close enough to smell, she saw what held it in place. It looked soft. A spongy rope. She didn't want it to be intestines.

But even as she contemplated the spaghetti lariat, she knelt then placed the slate on the ground, eyes fixed to it.

She paused to breathe. The man hadn't moved. And though she didn't dare check, she imagined his scrutiny hadn't left her. She imagined his tall and quiet focus had—

That's when it hit her. A small ripple of an idea. Barreling, growing in gusts of inklings and intuitions.

To Rei's puzzlement, she reached and retrieved a small, lumpy rock.

Before she could prod the flaws of her plan, she raked the stone across the gritty slate. The pressure to prolong. The pressure to please. Like when her parents handed her a paper and pencil at their rare parties, demanding minute masterpieces.

Her company in the woods seemed a bit worse.

But she also felt the pressure to survive, the desperation to live. It was her desperation that guided the stone. No frivolities or silly possibilities took up space in the forefront of her creative mind. She needed out. Out of the woods and away from the stinky, moist mask and the breathing beast behind it. She needed help.

Determined, she once again set stone to stone.

Again the slate delivered a less-than-charming translation. And all the more deviant as it rose into the air and erratically came to life.

Not a person. But it stood upright and short. A brutish, stocky figure with scaled flesh like the waves of the slate. And a drawn smile that had turned into a fanged frown.

Upon its involuntary birth, it stiffened and inhaled the dual-realm tension.

A carmine hand coiled around its throat. Rei pulled it toward him for inspection, glaring at its scaly flesh. Its body dangled from his grasp.

With a cavalier grip, Rei crushed the creature in his hands. Vertebrae mashed between his fingers, and its arms fell limp. Its window to struggle was short, then closed.

And witnessed by the motionless girl below.

The crushed creature was spared prolonged torture for a toll of saliva and blood that dribbled down

Rei's arm and slumped onto his filthy robe.

Spikes crashed to the ground, watered by the blood of the lifeless creature Rei had flippantly tossed against a spruce.

The back of Rei's nails tickled Lauren's cheeks as they opened to clasp her face. Sweat coated her numb feet, pooled in her hands. She didn't move.

An echoing crack broke the timidity of the forest. Even with just a glimpse, just a glance at something half appeared, Lauren could see her creation. Roark rotated and looked into her frightened gaze, claws delicately wrapped around her.

He vanished with—

No. His arm. He appeared fully, yielding to a merciless clutch. Rei's nails burrowed into his scaled forearm. Roark tried to teleport again, but the nails sank deeper.

Roark snarled.

The ground squirrels beneath them fled through contorted carvings and tunnels. And every bird left their perch. Wings flapped against their own bodies and those of others they collided with in aerial attempts to escape the dispute below.

Roark wrenched and wriggled.

No use.

The girl peered at his wounds, and he at hers.

Lauren's sudden trip from her apish liberator to the trunk that halted her flight with a thud didn't boast of much hang time. Through her diaphragmatic spasms, the girl lifted her head to witness the residual violence.

She pushed up but fell immediately. Frustrated at her tender, pensile arm.

She shimmied to a stand.

Foamy bubbles fell from jowls and onto the hooks clenched around Roark's throat.

The lone compensation for his suffering came when his claw sliced Rei's cloak and penetrated the flesh tucked behind the tattered fabric.

Without the instant drip of blood onto his hand, Roark would have conceded a miss—and a miss of the only shot he'd have. As it was, the lukewarm glop wasn't only welcomed but also granted him the opening he needed.

He wriggled free and dropped, escaping with a crack.

Rei's clawed graspings stopped after half an effort. Handfuls of air delivered news of failure. The mask bent forward slightly, the beast behind it bewildered. The world that lay through the stony portal was enigmatic enough to Rei without the disappearance and reemergence of the square-jawed primate. Captivating without the use of his uncharted sorcery, his teleportation.

Rei's pause wasn't calculating; rather, it was born of resentment. A new feeling of impossibility.

It was a river of jealousy. No, a flood of envy.

For Lauren, it was an opportunity to escape. And she took it. She rolled awkwardly into a stand and scrambled into the dark woods.

Perhaps the greatest disaster of Lauren's attendance that night was that it provided Rei the location Roark was aimed, rather than relying on where he was. Rather than having to predict.

Rei reset his focus and closed the gap between himself and the wounded girl.

It worked.

Roark appeared feet from Lauren's side. A congestion of royal fern, five feet high, became an unwitting and concealing accomplice. An aid to Rei and the ambush stroke that lacerated Roark's meaty chest.

But Roark retaliated, simultaneously lobbing potent blows and coercing Rei away from Lauren. His aim, however, was impaired, each unsuccessful jab leaving him vulnerable to Rei's maniacal hacks.

And Rei delivered with enthusiasm.

Peeled upward. Downward. As scaled flesh was torn from Roark's apish body, he felt his doom.

Not yet.

Fur too fine to notice topped paper-thin flaps. Bones shone through pliant skin. Claws tipped the translucence and clamped the assailing Rei inches from Roark's underbite. Bulging eyes instinctually delighted in the crumpled heap to which Rei's outer cloak fell and the fresh, matching holes that oozed liquid from his charred back.

An involuntary bond based on loyalty to their creator and an appetite for bloodlust was ripe enough to beckon the bat to the conflict. And its attempts to accentuate the damage, to open Rei's throat with its razored teeth, meant Roark was spared a killing stroke.

But the bat missed its second attempt—its jaw snapping short of making contact —and Rei abolished optimism for deliverance or triumph. A clasp of the bat's folded, scarred wing opened preexisting holes broader still. A prick into its back, its abdomen.

Roark wriggled, but his muscles refused. Defeat was bestowed in the collapses of blemished wings. Once powdered with snow, the ground mushed into a chestnut brown, and Roark glimpsed the bat's plummet to it from his peripheral vision.

Suddenly Roark's hamstring was punctured with a pop. A resonant wail from the ape. As if to highlight the brutality, Rei pulled a procured rock from Roark's leg and shallowly stabbed the nape of his neck.

But there was still a chance; the bat hadn't surrendered. It flapped awkwardly out of the clearing then back in, fending off its opponent with fitful floggings.

Roark rolled to his side, giving the bat a clear angle on Rei.

The bat's effort was more mayhemic than skilled combat. Still, it was agile enough that it quickly regained lost footing from a miss.

Although Rei wasn't nimble enough to counter each attempt with one of his own, he was adequately agile to redirect blows so he didn't catch the full force of the bat's claw-tipped wings and razor-sharp fangs.

The bat whirled in and out of the clearing, this way and that. It swiped, desperate to hinder its creator's assailant. But Rei was patient. He maintained his defensive game, committing more energy to dodging than striking.

He conserved his efforts until at last he caught the bat midflight, spun in one of its flurried attacks.

A limb was pulled from the bat and flung over Roark, spirting blood as it sailed through the air. Roark's flat snout slumped defeatedly to the ground. The bat's death had drained his final stores of adrenaline.

Conscious but only just. Only aware of deliberate, premonitory steps. Each step matched the drawn-out inhalations snuffled through Roark's snout, until they stopped near his side.

Rei knelt, dropping his fist as he lowered; it

cracked when it made contact with Roark's skull. Cherry droplets spat from the gashes on Roark's skull, released by pounding hands. He relinquished, but the thuds persisted. Loud and quick. Rei grunted as the woods hushed at the drumming of bony, closed fists. He was engrossed, eagerly bent for the conclusive thump. The wallop that would sanction a return to enshrouding silence. Only those deep, rapid thuds resounded.

And then it ended.

Breathing heavily, Rei knelt beside Roark. Blood trickled from the ape-like creature's legs. Poured out of his mouth. He wheezed faintly.

Rei reached to Roark to deliver the killing blow, but his hand gripped...nothing.

Roark had vanished.

He didn't make it far, and it had cost his abdomen dearly, but he appeared feet away in a tumble. He held his gut as closed as he could in an effort to limit the leakage.

Rei grunted and stretched, trying to eke out a conclusive grasp.

But Roark had vanished again. Only feet away. The separation between teleports waned. He crawled for extra distance, hocking a screech from his gashed throat. Like an impaled hog's petition, a bull elk bugle. His insides protruded, peeking from behind broken flesh. The contortions in his spine made lying down an insufferable pursuit, so he arched in agony.

The incisions the bat had bored into Rei's back didn't penetrate deep enough to be the reason for his paralysis. Yet his breaths were congested, as if to hinder their condensation in the frigid air. To conceal himself from a silhouette that emerged from deep within the woods.

The racket of Roark's misfortune seemed to register less to Rei, until it was nearly mute.

Haze enveloped skin in wisps. Skin that should have been filleted and marred. It encased capable legs, not the fragments he had salvaged. Legs that bolstered a blemished but restored frame.

The invalid he had shouldered and fed by hand had recovered. Without hesitation, he'd jeopardized himself to deliver her from her abusers. Yet her new pearl eyes wouldn't even look into his.

He'd bent all his thoughts on her. Guarded her. Hunted for her. He'd chewed scraps of meat and spat them past her broken jaw and down her raw throat, but her focus lingered on the slate as if she hadn't noticed him. He'd carried her as delicately as he could, trying to avoid added anguish, further injury. And suddenly she was in a more favorable condition than he.

And he didn't sense the same loyalty.

In the seconds that followed, Rei split his

attention between Roark and the newly restored Witch. The phantom who brazenly moved toward the slate as if not noticing the battleground or considering the possibility that there might've been more creatures aligned with the ape—or willing to sacrifice themselves to let the little girl escape.

The barbarism of the battlefield was a calm serenity compared to the pernicious damnation they'd portaled from, and The Witch seemed to take her time crossing it to the slate.

Some dozen yards away, Roark felt the abrasions, the blood that fell down his eyes blurring his vision. He saw Lauren holding her arm, running away. He saw the blood on the back of her legs as she fled. The dark blemishes on her arms.

Tremors drew through his furred, floppy ears.

The earth crumbled where he lay, downward and out, deep and to the sides, impelled toward the earth. It fragmented to the nearest tree, only relenting once it bisected half its height. Blood spattered and spilled into the impression's cracks.

Claws hooked around the bifurcated tree. Bark and wooden particles blew out in both large chunks and dust. The air was heavy with the splintered bits and escorted the massive tree to the ground, crashing through the neighboring branches.

Beneath the branches and pine needles and the aftermath of the rubbled spruce, Roark scrambled.

A ghostly escapee. He appeared feet away. A few feet farther. In bursts he split from the scene, slinging shards of the fallen tree in his wake.

The trees had thinned, as if cleared for the sole use as a battleground. And though The Witch withdrew from the warzone, Rei married his attention to Roark.

The shift of momentum was strangulating. The sway he once had—and the outcome of the fight he had solidified in his mind—dissipated. His head pulsed with despair. The damned ape and his capacity. His fascination escalated, his blood boiling with rage.

He could recall few memories. And so Rei recognized these inconceivables as one of those things: something he felt driven toward but knew better than to pursue.

Even as he witnessed how helpless the ape was in his efforts to reel and whisk away, Rei wouldn't chase him.

He knew his queries wouldn't be granted answers. So he never asked. Why the ape wouldn't succumb to the onslaught. Why he could gallivant through the air as if the snowy, blood-spritzed wind were his to govern.

How The Witch had returned mystifyingly contradistinct from the sufferer he had delivered, safeguarded.

Yes, this world was becoming more trouble than it was worth.

Suddenly the ape didn't matter: Observing them, outside their reach.

And once more Rei stood before the slate.

Without delay or rumination, or secrecy to hide their departure, he took a gray, all but transparent hand, and they portaled through the slate, leaving Roark and the woods behind them.

The grunts and sounds of the conflict had become vaguer. The sound of their movements was a combination that didn't belong. Something like the whir of a helicopter blade that had morphed into a carnivore's growl. These, and the report of ruptures, lacerations, and cracks, grew faint with the distance Lauren put between herself and the clearing. She moved through the ensnaring woods as quickly as she could.

Her cradled arm demanded attention. And adrenaline couldn't dam every tear and sob.

She overlooked the sounds of the woods. Grouse and wild turkey, feathers and flutters. Evading turmoil for the sky. The clopped shuffles of deer attempting to best the treacherous terrain. The surrender of a young spruce, betrayed by its waterlogged roots, felled by the reverberations of the scuffle.

Try as she did, Lauren couldn't ignore her arm drooping at her side. Nor could she decide whether to brace it to her body or hold it out, lest it jostle against her on her run. So she alternated, paying more attention to it than the shed as she passed it. The weathered shack that had commanded fear was now camouflaged by her tunnel vision and pressing pace.

She didn't consider the newly dismantled door. No note of the reflecting circles in the cracked window, solid eyes piercing through the portion she had wiped clear.

But she recognized something. And definitively. The landmark where she had lifted the slate. The only place where she had intentionally delayed. Where it had been positioned. Less slate than a fine-grained plaque. Feigned inanimacy.

The soil was still split, sunken. There was no blood, no evidence that much of anything had happened. Merely a depressed, cracked ground.

Could there be a chance any of it wasn't real? Possibility she'd dreamt it?

Maybe it would be okay; all right again, even after all of it. After she was punished and everything had settled. Yes, it might well be a long time, but it could be.

Back to normal despite the extraordinary things

that had happened.

Smoke bellowed in waves amid the pines clotted with brush. Lauren's hope that her life would return to the way it had been (or to some form similar enough) wafted away as the strange smoke glided in.

When did she lose her left shoe? Why had it taken her so long to notice? The ground felt uneven until she kicked the right one off as well. There. The missing shoe wouldn't trip her steps. She picked up a shaky sprint again, away from the creek, away from the smoke.

Finally.

She could see the driveway.

Her fear soothed a bit as she anticipated going home. Mildew and maltreatment, set atop cinder blocks. The warmth of her bed. A snuck spoonful of peanut butter.

Despite the relief, fatigue dripped an inky curtain down her eyes. A cruel mask of unconsciousness. Then light was partially restored in twinkles. Raven black again and then a sparkle. Each flicker of awareness was reprimanded by the narrowing blackness that confined it.

Fright fused with faintness. And then it didn't.

The woozy tempest had taken her attention... somewhere.

The big house again. Only for a second.

Somewhere else. Into a vehicle. Somewhere.

Somewhere pitch-black. A musty sack over her eyes.

Men barked at Lauren's father. He pleaded a little, but mostly he listened. As did Lauren under the dark bag. They told Mr. Bevill he should have hunted with intent, persistence. It would mean his own child as a substitute if he didn't.

The exchange frequented her dreams. Plenty of elements she couldn't decipher; nevertheless she knew the implications well enough. Like someone relaying confusing, imminent danger they had no intention to impede.

It was sweltering. A dreadful discomfort. She was somewhere loud. Deplorably loud.

But the mobile home was quiet.

Only cold, low-howling winds masked the sound of her pattering feet as her mind swirled back to the hardship at hand. There was relief at the end of her excessive, dismal run. Even her feet stung less. Desperation to simply be back in bed, to be afraid of and aggressed by the more familiar. The more predictable. Desperation for a choice, if only minor.

Selection of the thrashing belt's material and type perhaps. Not the easy choice one might think—more of a science of sorts. A metal clasp hurt worse, certainly. But the requisite number of thrashings fell to nearly single digits, conversely as the material softened, making it a worthwhile contemplation.

Or even the option of "Double or Nothing," if she was lucky, might be extended to her. A long shot, but the possibility warmed her.

And then it didn't. Nothing did.

Pain shot sharply from her back and along her spine. A peculiar breed of pain. Acute. Sudden. Agony, chased by paralysis and disorientation.

She hadn't heard anyone, seen anyone.

Her knees cracked in a plummet to the freezing ground and a thorny weed that lay disguised beneath the snow. Her exhalation spewed equally from the plunge and the twist. But also in defeat. Her damaged arm dropped cruelly to her side.

Serrated metal punctured through her back and stomach and shot a drop of blood to her purple toes.

FIVE

SOMEONE STEPPED INTO THE light.
A lamp hung from a corroded wire, attached to the side of its broken metal frame. With the wild nature of its swing, not to mention the mere twenty watts, the glass pear would have been of little use to a nimble, inquisitive mind. Much less to a young girl sporting a scraggy rabbit dress; blood filtered through an animated paw and down a fuzzy cotton tail, long since white.

A figure shifted in a dark, dusty corner of the shed.

An extension cord had been used to bind her, portions of its rubber coating damaged. The frayed wiring, a consequence of Mr. Bevill's careless and amateur grip on his power tools, composed a bouquet of pins to her back. The rushed knot loosened with her fidgets.

A gleam appeared, the golden-red hue of a Phillips head screwdriver—stocked in a first-available-space sort of way. A screwdriver within reach.

But Lauren prioritized the corner.

Feet scuffed grime like spackling paste into the floorboard's cracks and crevices. Their graduality flaunted composure.

Lauren tried to speak. Tried to cry "Mama," but she choked, interrupted by congealed globs.

It wasn't a delirious half howl for her mother. Nor was the figure that drew near the mirage she'd hoped for. Begged for in that split second—in the split second she tried to convince herself it was impossible.

Mrs. Bevill cleared cobwebs and insectile irritants. A knife sprinkled red drips to the floor, mixing with years of dust. Her eyes were focused. Angry. And scared. Wary, as if she faced the greater danger.

The light mocked the dismality with metallic grinds and sways that illuminated gargled, shallow inhalations. Wheezes limited by an arched spine. Ruby, foamy drools from a trembling chin. Alarm in wet green eyes.

Lauren felt weight, a heaviness from within. As though the remainder of her blood stores had gone tight and heavy in obstinance, fighting to stay inside.

A thought pricked her mind. If she hadn't wandered in the middle of the night, she'd still be at home. She wouldn't feel the freezing tremors that shook her body and forced the frayed wiring back and forth, abrasions forming on her skin.

In speculation and despair she conceived a sort of a remedy. She didn't think she'd quite solved it. Didn't think she could fully mend what had gone wrong. Yet a desperate idea consumed her.

I'll clean the whole house.

Her eyes closed on her tears. She ached to plead her promise aloud.

And then the good of it—her arm wriggled free from the hastily spun cord—was joined with the bad. Mrs. Bevill had noticed the screwdriver. What was worse, she'd seen Lauren's eyes hover briefly over it, evidently attentive to the oxidized metal and the liberation that slept in its flaky patches.

But the girl's thoughts were adrift; she was too preoccupied with sorrow to consider grabbing the tool.

Mrs. Bevill stood incredulous to her daughter's treason, floored she could consider harming her own mother.

When the disloyalty was too much to bear, she lunged.

Lauren pushed away the steel, frantic for distance between her aching stomach and the Santoku blade. Desperate to diffuse the situation and much too distracted to question what unnamed defiance she was guilty of.

She reached for the screwdriver without thinking it through. More of a defensive reflex than an intention to stop her mother. When she paused to reconsider, her mother acted.

The knife pressed through her tiny palm.

The screwdriver sat firmly in her other hand.

But she didn't use it.

She wanted to. To pry away the agony. To prod back the gloom. But fright steadied her hand.

Besides, she didn't want to misbehave.

The rage didn't leave Mrs. Bevill's watery eyes. Not even when she secured the screwdriver in her own hand.

Lauren bawled at the butchery, the betrayal.

The pointed, cross tip jammed into her chin. A spasm. Nerves jerked her mouth open but only to the width the screwdriver allowed.

As Lauren's head dropped to her chest, Mrs. Bevill crumbled to a near faint. The sodden floor and her cloggy snow boots doubled her burden to kick back from the barbarity. Until moisture dampened the small of her back. Wetted by the molded wood, straightened in disbelief. And in crippling dread.

What will they think of me?

There was only terse passivity after Rei and The Witch had gone. A subsistence of carnage that quickly yielded to the matured house fire. The strength of the flames broadcasted in snapping flares. Fire lit the coniferous encirclement, undressing the trees in uneven wafts.

And the slate lay slanted in a red bath, in the company of the bat.

Opalescent cloth danced against pale legs. Its edges singed as they grazed the conflagrant ground. The Witch's legs were blemished with bruises, some of which were decades old. The bare patches on a despoiled scalp had been replenished with enthralling waves of silver.

Her calves struggled to tighten despite the incline they traversed. Feet quivered on the blistering dirt below. The barbs that clothed the bluff tested her footing again and again.

But her muscles weren't the shreds Rei had salvaged from famished jaws. And as he climbed behind her, he contemplated her capability.

It was a world they knew. And the resonant

lamentation was an ambience they were accustomed to. It was the quiet of the crag Rei couldn't tolerate. The clarity of his steps and the scorched crackles of the ground. And whatever intellect he'd been bestowed, whatever understanding he'd been crafted with, a warning waned nearly aloud.

Yet he dismissed it, unwilling to contest his loyalty and stray from The Witch.

Perhaps unable.

The consequences were unclear if he accompanied her. But he felt certain what would happen if they were separated.

It had been a narrow escape the last time. And the risk was unpalatable. No matter how altered she'd become, how arcane. So, despite his wounds, he matched her pace.

Rocks and thorns crowded one another, more densely as Rei and The Witch neared the top of the crag. The rise grew steeper, up to a rocky structure wedged into the peak.

A corpse lay near its foundation.

But neither the bones nor the carrion crumpled beneath the flexion of long, clawed feet stilled the duo's gait.

A murky vapor settled deep into worn knuckles. Chipped lower canines flashed the shreds of flesh that dangled from them. A glance at scarred cheeks stained with drying blood, flaunting satiation with the body beneath him.

The Ghoul was markedly feebler than Rei presumed the tyrant of such perdition would be. His frame was bent, the extent of his wounds disguised by his slouch.

Rei considered him not for his condition or renown, but for his role in The Witch's misfortune. Yes, it was The Ghoul who'd given the order. Rei had heard the accusations hissed from the demons he'd interrogated and tortured upon finding the disfigured Witch.

A series of gnawing and grinding indicated little urgency as Rei approached. The Ghoul merely scanned the trespasser and chewed a gristly portion of flesh. And took but a brief account of a poorly veiled falter.

The gashes in his back were vents that leaked in trickles, as though life were fleeing Rei's impaled flesh. His attention bent to The Ghoul and the yellow eyes that shifted from Rei to the victim at his feet and back, as though he saw no difference between the two.

Rei felt no desire to provoke a conflict.

And then he did. At once, a loosed malice. An instinctive thirst for mutilation. Provoked by a minor shift in focus: a glance from The Ghoul to The Witch.

And so Rei lunged.

A hurl in devotion. A total loss of regard for all but the heave of his body and the thrust toward the repulsive hunchbacked king.

Despite their imbalanced skill sets, a faint optimism remained: anticipation that an order of retribution was imminent. Justice for the pitiless savagery that had been commissioned.

A memory of shredded skin dangling from gored, empty sockets flickered in Rei's vision. Damage spied from darkness, tracking The Witch much too late.

In that recollection, a quiver constricted his spine and emphasized the impossibility of her condition once again.

For she had white, seeing eyes. No plague of blindness.

She was beautiful to him. Inconceivably so, from just a glimpse amid his assault. The holes in her silken drapery didn't correlate with any leaking abrasions beneath them.

And then a single plunge.

One stroke, an interruption of remembrance and rumination.

Clumps of his flesh camouflaged the weapon, but it could have only been her. Yes, he was sure The Witch held whatever had punctured him.

Her allegiance had changed. An unthinkable alliance was now undeniable. He had suppressed the thought more than once. But of course—how else could she have recovered from such spoil?

The betrayal drummed a dismal ache in Rei. But the spike that impelled him was worse; it seared tissue and skin, infused misery and paralysis.

He stumbled backward, toppled, his hands pushing his body from the smoldering clay beneath him.

Wisps of thick vapor drew from his chest like smoke from a sulfur pit.

The beast scuffled to his victim. "What a sacrifice." Protruding teeth nearly nicked a notch in Rei's mask with the taunt.

With an ungentle clutch, he raised Rei's arm and amused himself with the deadweight of it, swinging it back and forth. Watching, feeling the hopeless sufferer.

"This world didn't birth you." The antagonizing lingered with cruel pauses.

The placid, tender manner with which he beheld the ground, the hellish world around them, was more than simple reverence. It was adoration. The Ghoul recognized the Age of Rei was expiring and spent its final moments as he wished.

The mask peeled, a ruddy sludge pinched callously between The Ghoul's fingers. "It won't mourn you."

It worked. This last taunt undermined whatever sliver of martyrdom Rei savored. A slouch demonstrated his defeat.

White eyes beheld the horror as The Witch followed The Ghoul's grip on Rei's shoulders. Stench and blood spurted freely as his claws wrenched them apart, exposing tender red flaps enveloped in a white coating.

Coarse, discordant screams were succeeded by ashen vapor. Remnants of a confiscated soul abandoned Rei and compressed into The Ghoul's fingertips, his body mending with its influence.

The Witch mulled the possibilities as broad splits in his hide filled. Maimed muscle sewn by some ghostly remedy. Panic pushed a thought. A thought that with his new countenance his oath wouldn't be honored.

But the pledge was upheld.

Steam accompanied the thick smoke surrounding their hands, traveled into her fingers and through her veins. A metamorphosis that ushered vitality in pulses through their clasped hands. The Ghoul caressed hers, a slight grin on his face. He enjoyed it: the drain, the ache. The disrepair in his own tendons as hers strengthened. The searing on his own flesh as hers tightened and scarred.

She was too apprehensive to observe directly, too anxious to make witnessing the unraveling obvious. But even peripherally the price he paid was evident, significant.

Vulnerability shocked The Witch from studying her repair. Somehow she'd missed The Ghoul's withdrawal from his peak. Of course such an oversight only emphasized how alone she was. Yet again.

It was a jolting truth. Like she'd been startled from those rare sleeps, stowed away in the shadows.

Blood and gray matter oozed from Rei's corpse and trickled between The Witch's feet and down the crag.

Despite the suffocating scares of that hellish world, a sensation almost too intense to tolerate slung its influence through muscle and bone. A might that was nearly familiar. Without needing confirmation, nor to explore, her strength felt obvious.

The alteration reached beyond the physical. Perspective was delivered on those velvety wisps. A side effect not intended by The Ghoul, the remedy broke her fixation and clarity took its place.

She paused at the top of the ascent. The implications of her newfound abilities formulated, augmentations that seemed to swell as each second passed.

As did the danger of lingering.

For better or worse, something had been dramatically altered. Without need for further prompt, The Witch dove from the slope, leapt from the promontory to the lakes of blood below.

And at the middlemost of her dive, she disappeared.

The most sizable sac in the room was smaller than the one he'd seen during his last visit. Not large enough for stretch marks to adorn the pliant vessel, but he had no choice.

The Ghoul pulled a foul, sludge-covered child from it, without delay for a proper, more complete birth. Nor did he waste any velvety vapor to plant another in an empty, neighboring sac.

There was no time. And no sense in denying how emptied he was of his vigor, his ability. How with each relinquishment of metaphysical sway, his deterioration seemed even more severe.

A glance around the room of mostly empty sacs confirmed his suspicions that his world wasn't doing its part. It wouldn't be enough. Besides, the cultured spirits were simply fragments, splinters of recycled souls. As were the souls of the imps he lured with the children. They were weathered, but had no choice in their nature. Being bred from the hellish world itself bent their behavior. And so their souls were counterfeit. A manufactured sort of wicked. Less than adequate.

A real soul took time. Testing. It took circumstance and influence for it to harden and decay. Besides, the flesh of a demon was nearly repulsive with its monotony alone.

When the conjurers had enticed him with their chance, reckless development of a portal (not to mention their rudimentary, revealing enchantments), he'd found a great source of decayed souls.

Earth. A world of morals perversed by choice.

The Ghoul yearned for them, chased the taste. In every colony of their world, vessels of putrid spirits lay unwitting and ripe in delicate bodies. And he wallowed in his gluttony.

But the summoners and witches observed their mistake. Assessed the unbridled wreckage.

He had no loyalty to their agenda.

So fell their expulsion, claiming The Ghoul's exile as the fruit of their witchcraft.

But it was no more than an accident in their panicked, portal tamperings. In their undisciplined, fanatical enchantments and potions and sacrifices. Still, it worked and his attempts to return to earth had been thwarted ever since.

But The Witch had followed him, devoted to his malevolence from the moment she had beheld him.

He knew human flesh, tasted their souls. Their double-dealings, their personalities granting energy in his lustful consumption. Yes, The Witch had followed. Loyalty in the act alone.

But she too had betrayed him.

No. She had created Rei from fear of her new hellish hearth and assisted his escape through the portal, but she'd reformed in her agony. In repentance she had brought Rei to him. Yes, and she would remove their concealed obstruction on the portal, reverse their incantations. He was sure of it and relieved his reliance on her would soon come to an end.

Besides, until her disposal alleviated all possibility of rebellion, no further Reis could be developed. No rescuer pried from the slate's surface.

None, at least, heavy with talent or capability. She'd become too tainted. Formerly corrupted, at present a part of his amoral abyss down to the molecules.

The might and mastery of those birthed by the slate were assembled by the fusing of good and evil, so he dreaded no attempts she might make to manufacture another.

He stabilized himself in the gooey scarlet tunnels, towing the wailing child underneath the structure. Down the spine of his crag and into a cave of sorts. A swamped cavern.

Whatever the liquid was, it was sufficiently contaminated to paint a thick residue on his ankles. And just deep enough to stifle the childlike being once he plopped it into the cavern's pollution. It spat and choked and swiped at a thorn-covered root here and there, radicels that seemed to belong to the mountain itself.

While The Ghoul was dexterous enough despite his disrepair to bend the tangled collection for balance, the roots that dangled from ceiling to muck were of little value to the child he had discarded. Its uncooperating, frail grip failed. Over and over until...

A floating collection of mold and rancid guts. The child grasped as it sailed by. Still, a pathetic clench on the slimy intestines was little more than placebic. No help to manage an inhalation, much less to balance.

The Ghoul climbed, lifted himself above. A delectable vantage, his back to the ceiling of thorny veins. The child's cries rang throughout the dark entanglement, signaling potential passersby.

Before the trap was more than a few minutes old, it had been sprung. Something or someone had slipped deep into the shadowy encirclement. Reverberations and sniffs without vigilance. Slushy footsteps attached to a scrawny demon. He stopped, barely able to catch his breath, as the child floated into view.

He hadn't been followed. No, a swift scan assured him his assumption was correct. He was alone. Aside from the whimpering infant.

His caution dissipated, driven out by starvation. So he walked on, unable to pass on such a treat.

The child squealed and squirmed, but the imp quieted it quickly. Smart to kill before that rapacious first bite. An even more astute calculation would have been to sprint with his meal. Better yet, to have absconded once he'd seen it, or to have never passed the penumbra, the shadowed boundary that braced the mountain.

The imp howled, dragged on his by his ankle, a victim of an aerial assault.

He popped out of the water. In again. And back out.

Broken wheezes for air, at the benevolence of what lurked and aggressed. The window through which to see, the moments his eyes peeked above the squalid basin, was short. But enough. Time enough to spy vertebrae straining the threadbare patches of a dark cloak. A stooped frame. Long, thin arms. Time enough to tremble at his certainty.

Time enough to see his calf being torn from his body; then The Ghoul consuming it with one hand, dragging him with the other.

He wished it was his head that had been cleaved from his body.

It would be a slow death.

Tongues of fire tested their limits, slithering toward the nearly dismantled shed. Mrs. Bevill lay curled, cowering and immobilized beside a toppled bucket of rusted tongue-groove and needle-nose pliers.

But it wasn't the forest heat, or the hindrance as the blaze nearly blockaded the doorway, that reinforced her paralysis. No, it was the flames' unknown origins that stopped her. Stilled her impulse to avoid the impending inferno.

Above all, it was the puddle that kissed her boots. Droplets from her daughter's impaled jaw.

Splinters shot from the edge of the weathered door, torn from its rusted hinges.

Mrs. Bevill grunted, "Who... Wha...?"

A colossal wrinkled head wielded an underbite and turned the corner. With barely a tilt, ruby-red beads—accrued in ample jowls—descended in a grizzly drizzle.

He huffed through his scrunched nostrils and smelled the whiffs of the aftermath.

Mrs. Bevill could merely watch, terribly aware she couldn't write this off to delirium.

A racking jounce of awe and affright.

The crunching, clattering. Audible in his every movement. Like a mantis manipulating its mandibles.

Her hands clamped over her mouth, suppressing a squeal as she noticed his hand on his side. And the guts that squeezed and slithered between his claws, thwarting his attempts to hold them in. She could smell their putrid, fecal odor.

Sharp shoulders bent forward, and his head bobbed slightly in his investigation. He sniffed, wiping his face with one hand. A sequence of tilts steered his head as he studied a chair, stools, and tools that were tossed about. Pieces of glass from shattered things on the floor. All dusted with blood.

But he seemed to have suspended any real fury. Until his bulging eyes caught a petite body in a puddle of filth. Slumped in a pile of blood and urine. Contorted precariously.

Mrs. Bevill caught the way he pushed his side and shifted his body to avoid leaking onto Lauren. He hadn't blinked, and he seemed not to breathe as he leaned over her corpse.

Then at once he lifted her, maneuvering his claws deliberately, lest he scrape her skin.

Mrs. Bevill stared with wide eyes. A creature from a horror film. Perhaps the Devil, come to punish her for killing her child. She stared in awe, transfixed in the mania.

It was either the sharp inhalation or the scuff of her feet that induced Roark's attention. He gently laid Lauren back on the splintered floorboards.

"No... I-I just..." But what do you say to a demon? What do you plead to such a beast?

Concern for moral duty couldn't have been in his large head. Surely not. No, but her confessional became screams just the same. She said she was sorry. In so many rephrasements she apologized, reasoned, panicked, pleaded.

She referred to her often-forgotten religion and conjured whatever names and prayers she could muster. They morphed into an indecipherable collection of gut-wrenching bargains.

Roark's claws pierced her leg, and she heard a snap as they cleared the bone.

She writhed.

But not on the shed's floor. Her stomach dropped, and suddenly she fell to the filth of the forest, the freezing dirt.

The clasp tightened.

Her head throbbed and whirled. Triangles monopolized her vision.

Roark pulled violently, with purpose.

Another jolt and she rolled with the pain. Reached for anything to interrupt the torment. Nearly grasped a stone for defense or perhaps just to interrupt the drag. A slate-like rock.

The beast seemed to reach for it as well. Yes, he bent to it. Touched it. And—

Without warning she contorted. A cruel mangling midair. She saw triangles again, but more. All shapes. And colors. She felt the air granulate and her screams go raspy with the dust.

As though she were on the most unbearable roller coaster, she was spun into the air and dropped harshly. Blinded aside from stray shapes and the most astounding colors streaking past her as she lurched this way and that.

And screams. Screams roaring from wherever they'd traveled to. Screams she'd never heard. More mortifying than she thought conceivable in their roared, ceaseless retches.

The atmosphere stifled her lungs, but it wouldn't kill her.

A jolt.

The distress became less disorienting but no less severe. She tumbled with its sudden stillness, limited by the beast's grip on her, like a dog tethered to an abusive master.

They emerged in a thick fog. Indifferent to her tribulation and determined in his objective, he lugged her.

Despite the sting radiating from her leg, Mrs. Bevill directed her attention ahead. The shadow fell like a discarded veil. Hues of red dissolved the contoured lines and polychromatic patterns that had ambushed her eyes.

If only for its massiveness, the place might have been mesmeric. If not for the savagery that painted it in thick, cannibalistic, nefarious coats. The pollution of indiscriminate ravishment.

Wherever a cluster of stones had formed, a body lay mangled. Wherever a gap lay between carcass and unholy ground, a set of eyes peered toward the shadow barrier.

Those who'd not spied the apish beast and his wailing treat went about their egregious tasks undisturbed. Molestation for the routine obscenity of it rather than savage arousal.

The depredation took an odd pause when the giant came into full view. The sight of such a massive creature was enough to still the methods of despair and behavior of millennia.

They were too craven to approach him but too intrigued with the flesh he lugged to not inspect within limits.

Beside the apish demon's spiky claws through her arm, and a blemish here and there (not to mention the vomit coating her formfitting dress), his prisoner was fresh. Untouched and welcome.

Mrs. Bevill wheezed, unable either to suffocate or breathe. Hopelessness down to her cells, which must have considered melting just to put an end to it.

She had witnessed enough in the short time

they'd lived in New Sagres City to convince herself that hell, or something like it, might exist.

The first week in the woodland home had spurred peculiar nightmares that were as clear as memories. The accounts of catastrophe didn't seem to bother her much (terrible ghost stories promulgated far too long by bored nonthinkers. Kids went missing; it wasn't special to New Sagres). And the accusations they'd escaped with their relocation were outdated and childish (the bishop *has* to have depraved intentions with children).

But she knew something was wrong from the start. That day her husband snapped the curt "We're leaving" back at their old house.

That stupid black fucking phone. Fucking visits from strangers in charcoal fucking suits. Meetings he forbade she even allude to.

She should have said something long ago. Or left.

But she couldn't have been nearly as culpable as the perpetrators, even if her husband was guilty as accused. Maybe horrible things had happened, probably worse than she imagined, but she couldn't be responsible. To keep quiet couldn't be the same as to commit the crime.

And sure, she had killed her daughter.

But she was about to lose it all. Square one all over again. Once more people gave a fuck. Finally. Even the cops. At least her cop. And who knew who else? People would be attentive, interested in her comfort once more. The municipality, the congregation. And not just her church and not just other congregations. People in neighboring cities might even come together to console her. The whole county would know her story and want to help her. Wouldn't they?

Her heart sank at the absurdity. The happy-ending-less stories told of few rescues. This created a sense of angst among neighbors, not loyalty and friendship. She'd been blinded by optimism.

But her thoughts couldn't drift anymore. Not in that vile world. Not there. Not with them.

Sure, she was wrong. On some level or another, even immoral.

But the hell she was assigned to was more wicked, far more perverse than imaginable. Worse than she'd conjured in her sleep or in daydreams of her worst phobias. Surely worse than warranted.

The retraction of the beast's claws sent her body harshly to the ground. When she'd recovered, breaths surrounded her, humid and rank of bile.

Licking lips. Cracking, flickering fingers. The demons converged on the foreign being, momentarily too cautious to touch her.

When Mrs. Bevill was cast to the ground, the demons knew the beast didn't want his prize and began to permit themselves elation.

With the apish creature's egress, a single demon braved the hesitation. A piece of skin on Mrs. Bevill's stomach pinched between his fingers. He inspected and pulled, sluggishly tearing flesh from her side, before she registered her moans, before she could verify the banquet of misery was certainly too unbearable to be a dream or hallucination.

One grabbed her hands, satisfying himself with the flavor of her fingers. Another grabbed her hair and tugged at the obnoxious barricade to his food.

The filth of the darkness, had it been able to penetrate his anger, would perhaps have given Roark cautious pause. Serrated thorns were swathed in snagged flesh. Devils scattered this way and that, all trying to both flee and commission death. Mutual carnage. He knew evil lived beyond the portal slate and instinctually felt it to be a bridge to misery. But he hadn't anticipated such a foul extent.

And he was well enough aware without the pungent reminders that, without a remedy he would soon join the putrefying number of dilapidated corpses that plugged the shadows.

His odds of survival improved only faintly upon his seeing a white-eyed figure hurrying opposite his course, journeying the shadows he'd infiltrated only moments before, maneuvering with total preoccupation. He watched it closely, charting its course as much as his fatigued body and jaded judgment allowed.

Then the figure was gone.

And when it was, he crawled to where it had crawled from, avoiding what it had avoided.

Very quickly on the brink of being lost, he stumbled to the edge of the shadows then stood.

Blood trickled from the ground like sap from a spruce—a film on the eroded mount, trailing from where the figure had fled.

He pursued with bleak interest.

The puny, macabre ration of his former opponent atop the crag clouded his deliberations even further. Rei's formidable body was small, shriveled, and mutilated atop the hill's rubble.

He noticed something else oddly out of place when he drew close. Something he hadn't caught before. His eyes fixated on Rei's uncovered face. Not the face of the demons to whom he'd fed Mrs. Bevill.

Nor the skin. Not the wilted flesh of the more bantam residents.

Scales. Like the bat creature. Like his own.

"A disobedient creation." A few scraps of flesh dangled in gaunt, weathered hands. "Pried from a flawed portal. Loyalty bound too tightly to its creator." He wrung the flesh in his hands like a rag. Stressed his words.

Roark propped himself upright. From The Ghoul's failing gait, he intuited that he was off his game. And off guard for sight of the apish brute. Almost assailable.

The ground was saturated with thick slop from Roark's wounds, his interest in a scuffle fading with his drainage. His striped eyes were too heavy to concentrate. Breaths were pulled with profound strain.

Rei's flesh mask fell from The Ghoul's hands. "But it's been corrected. Rectified by the insubordinate herself."

He had his own labored breaths. And his efforts to close the distance between them weren't less demanding for him than they were for the meddlesome primate.

Even if Roark could have deciphered the cryptic ramblings, his attention was elsewhere. As he studied the remnants of his former opponent, the briefest recollection flickered.

It was The Witch, though he couldn't have known what title she'd been given. But yes, it was she who had crossed him in the shadow. It must have been. It was she who inadvertently had charted his course. The second half of the duo he'd spied from the trees, from the bushes on earth, who had stolen away from that decisive clash in the woods.

He tried to cultivate counterfeit interest in The Ghoul but couldn't sever his scrutiny from The Witch and her inevitable destination. As sure as he was that she was owed some blame for Lauren's demise, he was convinced the ghostly entity that had maneuvered the darkness wouldn't linger in that intolerable realm.

And after all, it was she who had chased Lauren.

Yes, and the seconds were precious.

Rancid seepage, the openings in his side. His body was failing. The Witch had lengthened the distance between them, while The Ghoul closed in on him. If he were to defeat him, it would have to be quick. Sudden. With his failing body, and an unfamiliar foe, only a surprise would do.

The ape hung his head.

The Ghoul relished in the lament, the perished decor on his hill. As he approached Roark, the smile that twisted across his mouth and through his dripping fangs dissipated. Golden eyes widened with rare concern.

"Scale skin," he hissed.

But he spoke to no one, and his puzzlement escalated.

A delayed crack sounded, marking the unwelcome shift within his inferno.

He hurt.

No, this was worse.

And he was a witness to the attack, a defenseless outsider to his own body. Observed the ape's disappearance, reemergence, clawed onslaught, then vanishment again.

He materialized near him. Too near him. Roark's barrage was brief, and he was gone again.

Again Roark appeared and attacked, each time leaving The Ghoul doubly damaged.

The Ghoul was wrathful at the pain. It shouldn't have been tolerated. His unholy world should have warned him. But it hadn't.

Trammeled in his own dominion.

As his neck tightened from a final assault, his head compelled to ascend, his back collapsed, he silently cursed his kingdom.

A dark purple blanketed the sky and spiraled over the mountainous mass—pitching particles of filth, morseled demons, fragmented rocks, thorns.

The atmosphere, the world entire, was reactant to The Ghoul's ruin, though whether mourning, enraged, or merely disturbed, Roark couldn't decipher. He studied his victim amid the tempestuous feedback.

The Ghoul's dark, smoky vapor forsook him. It wound through the air and spiraled toward Roark. Not stirred by the wind.

Despite the storm, it fastened to him. It clung to

its new host, a parasitic intertwining with his body from traumatized head to broken toe. Roark wiped at the intruding fog. Moved to be free of its enveloping steam as gusts of foul air persisted, heaving debris at him. Although he shifted and swerved, the vapor fastened relentlessly to him.

His crude shuffles were ineffectual. Flickering forward didn't work. Not even a teleport, partnered with an irritated huff.

The vapor permeated him in inescapable currents.

The damage was extensive, and they grew bored of her failing body.

Mrs. Bevill's open mouth rippled to the influence of violent trembles. Yet she was arrested by muteness. The split in her cheek ran from her chin to the bottom of her left eye, allowing an even more spacious aperture. But still her wails were inaudible.

The hell she was in kept her awake. Mercilessly aware.

Her left hand grasped at those clutching her throat, swiping with no sway on their strangulation. Blood poured from her eyes and mouth. It trickled past contaminated hands and their unhurried riving, pulling her jaw in half and passing the task of

torment to the world itself. For as the imps abruptly departed in nonuniform scurries and scampers,
her soul sank between the cowardly retreats. Ashy
smog, it spilled over rocks and serrated thorns. And
ducked under the drags of a single set of approaching, clawed feet and into the sweltering soil.

The largest claws on Roark's feet crooked like
talons. They grazed the residual scraps of Mrs.
Bevill's corpse as he stepped without contest or
concern of contest. Cloaked in a gray vapor.

His guts had ceased their seeping desertion, and
he now possessed an intense, deliberate countenance. Density anew. And the demons took notice.
They recoiled from the beast, cowered behind
crudely stacked decomposing corpses.

Twinges, remnants of wounds previously sus-
tained, panged their acute reminders. But he could
move. Or move well enough. Well enough to maneuver past the treacherous plants and toothy, chasmic
traps. Well enough to find the slate.

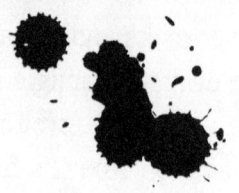

SIX

THE CRACKS OF THE woodland fire echoed in powerful snaps. The shed sat like a ship in the middle of the ocean, the approaching flames like impending waves, winding up to come crashing down and engulf its prey. A can of uncapped paint thinner tempted their descent.

The polluted air inside the Bevills' shed cracked as Roark appeared, his eyes fixated on Lauren and the screwdriver spiked through her chin and into her mouth.

The rouged hickory splashed with his steps.

He moved slowly. Determined. Altogether indifferent to the cataclysmic fallout and the booming soundtrack behind him. Not even as the fire latched to the door and scaled the weathered wood and the frame it had sat so precariously inside for years did his concentration falter.

The fire inched its way along the ceiling to the can of paint thinner and a jar of rank homemade insecticide.

Roark bent to his little friend. The thick pads on his palms spared her corpse from further puncture. The lumpy veins in his forearms tightened with his rage. Though perhaps not primarily, his indignation swelled with the knowledge that the inflictor was dead, not left to punish. He felt careless about the finality of his condemnation.

In caressing flutters, his vapor swaddled her. As he carefully withdrew the screwdriver, barricaded blood made its seeping escape.

Shovel-shaped jowls brushed Lauren's face as the flames reached their prize. Teamed with the paint thinner and other chemical allies, they spread throughout the shed, laying waste to all but an elusive monster and his fallen friend.

There was no mistaking the sound. Not since its previous thundering had granted them such a delicacy. The imps salivated at the possibility...and waited, like swine craving feed.

The woman was spent. They had torn, severed, consumed, and molested every parcel available.

But Roark didn't deliver.

No, and he pulled Lauren closer to him. Her arm had been torn, strained with his teleports. He wouldn't risk further disfigurement.

The air was scorching but different. It seemed to soothe whatever wounds the clouded smoke hadn't mended in his body. Or perhaps it simply delivered a sensation unique enough to undo the monotony of his aches. And only scantly. But he welcomed even the most minor modification to his discomfort.

The turbulence that had thrashed the crag began to break. And the loathsome world was quiet. Conceivably for the first time. The Ghoul's death had gifted the inhabitants a chilling recess in which even the most aggressive took to hiding.

Through waist-high, foul water, Roark sludged opposite the demons.

No beasts marked his trudges through the concoction of blood and excrement and worse. Decaying corpses of children lay on the hellish water's bank, shredded and spread like mulch.

Roark traipsed through vine and briar. The back of the crag was sure to be even less traveled, with its ridges and steep rises and frequent scorching rockslides. So he gripped a ledge and heaved Lauren to a gap in the crag.

His claws clamped shards of stone that protruded from an unreliable ledge. Pebbles and brittle blocks of cliff dislodged and fell, signifying what could be expected from a misstep, an over or underestimation.

The next ledge. And the next. Over and over. Roark's back pulsated pitilessly with each alternation of scaling and precise placement.

Until, at last.

He collapsed atop the summit. And dragged an obstinate breath.

Even as he indulged in a rest, slow inhalations snorting through his flat nose, Roark stayed attentive. Stayed quiet. Alert.

Echoed wails had softened to grumbles. And the stone structure, in all its dilapidated magnificence—and those sufferers hidden within its rancid rooms—kept silent to the change taking place atop the crag.

A pall of gray vapor settled onto Lauren's body.

Her nose twitched with its tickle.

Roark tipped his head, angled to focus. A second twitch moved her eyebrows. Just a bit. More than enough to prompt Roark to kneel over her, to poke her bruised shoulder, his enthusiasm tampered by gentleness.

But she lay otherwise motionless.

Until...

Another rustle. Her toe this time.

Roark didn't investigate the active haze that

enwrapped her corpse. Instead he stood and analyzed the condition of the summit.

Toiling on impulse, he limped inside the structure, gingerly carrying Lauren.

A room. Isolated. Small.

If she *did* wake, the broken bodies and decomposing corpses would be beyond unsuitable.

As he lay Lauren tenderly on the floor, an exhalation from the little girl suggested such an impossible revival.

He pitched lighter carrions brutishly down the humid hallway. Dragged the heavier, sundered imps into adjoining rooms. As good as it could be in such a hurry. If only before she woke he could—

A hastened hypothesis sent him kneeling to Lauren's side. Of course. How had he not noticed?

Pale silver had swaddled her in slow drifts from the shed's warped floorboards. It had wrapped her broken bones and abraded skin as he had toted her up the bluff and into The Ghoul's lair.

He caressed the gash in her stomach. Her fractured forearm. With cruel sluggishness, his vapor deserted him, kissed Lauren's contusions, and exacerbated his innumerable aches.

Their obstruction gone, his intestines resumed their painful escape.

His arm, his maimed head. The throbs came back nearly full-fledged.

But his focus was on his friend. The fact that the smooth cloud could have been absorbed at all was plenty to marvel at.

Timid eyes peered from adjacent quarters. Beings grateful to be overlooked in Roark's haste, yet not optimistic as they considered the apish intruder.

Roark stopped and stood.

Not remedied as he'd been with The Ghoul's persuaded generosity. But not quite the ruination as at the hands of the dismembered dissenter strewn across the bluff's peak.

Nevertheless he had stopped and stood. And without consideration of welcoming her to the mausoleum, he vanished.

The momentum of millennia had been stalled. Routine brutality and tumult abruptly halted. The grievous enforcer simply...gone.

The demons barked their confusion. But their howls trailed.

Steps ruffled from the murk. Coming toward them, not retreating deeper into it.

Then silence again.

Petrified, the demons peered. But for several minutes no one emerged.

A single demon saw to it that the struggle

between fear and intrigue registered at least one victory for the latter and crept toward the darkness.

But before it entered the thick mist, the holes on its leathered nape revealed to those gawking behind it the tips of long, black claws. And following: a blood filled, lackadaisical discard.

There came a panic, not by any means aloud, about the ape. A silent, confused gripe.

A frustration fidgeted within him as well. Roark huffed. He glanced toward the hilltop, and then he was gone.

His teleporting marksmanship placed him but a foot behind the closest demon, whose throat Roark stripped from its frail frame.

The sky uneasily witnessed a mutilation of its world's inhabitants. A coral blockade paused over the winnowing.

Pandemoniac motions sent his opponents into the dusty air and crashing to the ground. Flung across scorched bedrock and split down the middle from nose to rib.

Roark soaked in carnage and contention, the ruin invigorating him.

A gust of foul wind flapped his ears.

Despite his renewed disrepair, none had equaled his power. Nor could they maneuver the air as he could. He'd met none who had demonstrated such capacity. Except, it would seem...

The Witch.

Even more of a nightmare than Rei, than the hunchbacked Ghoul, if only for her inscrutability. Roark's mind snapped to the enigmatic threat. A threat he couldn't risk.

There must have been some relation that he hadn't put together, some connection he didn't care to. If his attention, his *intention*, was aimed at anything other than securing Lauren's safety, it would have been a slight satiation for his retributive bloodlust.

He threw in and out of a teleport, seized the slate by its tapered borders, and disappeared again.

His health was beyond inadequate to challenge The Witch. So he resorted to stabs and slashes in an attempt to destroy the slate and blockade any return on her part.

Hands jeered toward it; he tried again. Again. And again the slate was struck but impervious to the assault. No chip or blemish. No spoil from being cast against boulder and rubble and bone.

He teleported once or twice more, if only to put more distance between the stone and his napping friend. But the bulk of his strength was guided through jabs and blows to the stone itself.

With only a few warps, he was far enough to discover a new element: isolation, the cliff a speck to his lined eyes. No mauled creature or deformed demon. Only the secluded decay of the ground it-self, collapsed into shallow, trench-like valleys.

He spied a dead, rotted stump, its sides shriv-eled and hard, as though it had petrified mid-wilt. Equally dead was the ground around it.

And roots. They hung to the ancient trunk. And they too were plagued with thorns wherever they poked above the soil.

An idea struck him. Not good enough, but his choices were slim.

In fact, the decision had been made for him. The doom of it was emphasized in the settling destruc-tion and the hanging wall of an orange sky. His head rose to it.

Resigned to catastrophe and lack of choice, all at once Roark stashed the unbroken link. Laid it between the stump's roots. Lest another brave a thousand miles of isolation, and—whether good or misfortune—stumble upon it.

He flinched at the thought of facing The Witch in such comparative frailty. But only a half flinch. Any delay was squander, and a cost to the girl if nothing else. And not intervening, or any variation of it, was no choice at all. So he stroked the resil-ient slate.

Roark's portal to earth didn't come with pause or a lull to get his bearings—and it didn't come with peace. But nor did the flames overwhelm him. For before they had the opportunity to engulf him and sear his scales, a tackled embrace jarred his spine and took him away.

Flakes of vinyl and gypsum scratched his face and cut his skin. Fibrous plastics and glass were equally uninvited yet insistent, provoking Roark's temper as he burst through the wall of the mildewy mobile home.

The side of his abdomen had opened with the flight, which happened more and more with each teleport. His mind thrashed about, his brain rattling as though it would be loosed from his skull at any second.

He tried to strike and lash in the brief interludes in their teleports. During the first, his left arm was crushed and snapped, from scuffed elbow to pointed shoulder. During the second, the claws on his right hand plunged into The Witch's ribs. But with the third, his face grated against the stinging freeze of the woods' floor.

Then he was hoisted far into the air, heaved by his chest as he peered to the ground. Until it was gone.

The tingling in his abdomen twisted in a freefall. The air was even cooler now. A cold formerly unbearable, he now felt indebted to. It kissed his wounds, his deteriorating scales, his unobstructed drainage as he plummeted eighty feet.

He saw the deep dark of the sky. The dim tinge of the shirking moon. The few persistent clouds accentuated by flames that had scaled the evergreens. Tips of the gorgeous giants, attentive from below despite their own blazing misfortune.

On his back he fell through the air and looked to his side, only able to observe the havoc.

And the razor-wire bed awaiting him below.

When he thudded to the ground, the wire embraced him with an insidious slice through his leg, the bone and flesh of it abandoning his body. It lacerated the wrinkles on his face. Claimed an ear. Buried into his back.

His head was propped a bit by the dreadful barbs. With its assistance, he could see The Witch's white eyes. Her capable condition.

He wanted to lift his arm or leg, if only to see where he really stood. If only to know for certain. But the razor wire that cleaved him wouldn't unshackle. And it punished him for his exertion, widening his wounds.

Roark grimaced at the impedance in his palm. In his thigh. The sour taste that lingered in his underbite.

From the edge of the woods, The Witch blankly

soaked in the disassembling. And then she was gone, condensation lingering from her breath.

Then suddenly...

He had teleported plenty but never like this. His side ruptured worse still, hand severed, and the remnant stump of his leg tugged with their movement.

At once it was the air that vanished.

Water plummeted into his scrunched nose and mouth. He tried to move but couldn't. Even if his body wasn't destroyed, more than half now lay imprisoned in unyielding sludge, pinned in the bed of the Bevills' lake.

The Witch's silhouette wrenched closer then hesitated as she peered into the murky teal. The pins and needles had crawled to his head. They nauseated his leaking abdomen and stung his striped eyes. And he suffered their pitiless bites.

His body fell to the mercy of the water, almost seeking its approval to surrender. He pleaded for permission to rest, begged for the liberty to quit, his sight narrowing to a close.

The cold water taunted in relaxed ripples across its surface. Restrained him as The Witch withdrew, the wooded flames glowing through its waves.

Lauren's palms lay flat and closed slowly to her sides, feeling the jagged grooves and gooey grime beneath her as they slid. The scent of her pillow drifted into her nose. Warm blankets in a freezing room, after an all-too-rushed shower.

Her body, sore from a hard day of play, would sink into her mattress. Her toes would frisk the dirt granules from the day before as she swept her restless feet back and forth. Her mind, momentarily unconfined by familial stresses, would go blank with contentment. Weightless. Heavy. All at once.

She slowly opened her eyes and lurched.

She wasn't in the shed.

Trembling, emaciated bodies were twisted and timid. Yellow and red eyes darted up and down, keeping their contact with her brief. They didn't approach her, didn't move. Their cracked skin ached for moisture, anything but the dried blood in which they were ornately coated.

They were women. Or something like it.

She noted a particular sadness. Misery.

Whatever ghastly place she'd woken in wasn't hospitable to them, and they had no sway over it. She trembled at the implications.

She wanted to look to her own state but didn't want to risk jostling the placidity of the noxious room. But when she saw their anxiety, their cowering frames, she peaked at her own body.

At her arms, her legs. Dense and healed. Different. She was strong and felt it in the tenseness in her joints, the pinch in her muscles.

She could see it. A dark ashy hue to her skin, like the odd patches in her father's hair.

A light of sorts peeked from one of the adjoining rooms, as though it knew someone was eavesdropping. Someone who didn't belong.

Her upbringing had warned her in situations like this: in the frightening and foreign, you stay put. Stay quiet if you want to lessen the punishment.

But it didn't matter what she did, really. Her years of inadvertently testing a theory of inevitable pain had come to a close and finally a doleful realization.

Avoidance was punished as cowardice and attempts to usurp, manipulate. Yes, even obedience wasn't safe. Justifications were commonly issued following those lashings brought about by her parents' misjudgment or error: "Well, if you didn't do it this time, this is for all the times you disobeyed and didn't get caught."

Perhaps that was why she climbed to her feet and left the humid chamber.

And maybe it was the knowledge that her own mother had stabbed her—that harrowing glare in her eyes—that lessened the blow of the room's decor.

She should have been terrified. Should have collapsed at the grotesqueness of the blood, the severity of the women's wounds.

But she had a most alien moment of indifference.

Caught up in an animated curiosity, she approached a break in the wall. She eyed terrain, the likes of which she'd never seen or imagined. Knolls that had bulged and cracked. Miles of trenches cluttered with spikes like mammoth shards of glass.

The most vast, golden sky.

Her eyes scanned from one impossibility to the next until they reached a smoky encirclement below. It choked the mountain, the cliff on which she'd been set.

Even from her perch, it was clear wherever she was had turned on itself. The annihilation swelled with the pressure of circling, rusty clouds above.

The desire for a better vantage was promptly spent. And the strength that pulsated through her veins didn't feel adequate to vanquish such a nightmare.

A tear dripped from her soft, gentle face.

Angst clasped her. The worry that—no, the certainty that—no matter what happened next, she wouldn't be helped through it.

Suddenly she saw a man—multiple men—as clear as she'd seen them that autumn evening.

A memory concealed for years chose the most

horrific ambience in which to demand to be re-watched. Relived.

She felt their grip. Knew it was she herself who had shouted the throat-rupturing shrieks but couldn't help wanting to comfort. To answer the pleading.

Their glowers drilled briefly, before she had pried her eyes to scuffed, black sandals. Embarrassed. Ashamed.

The stench of their musty, unbathed bodies slouched behind slacked robes and drove into her button nose.

The kick made her shin throb. She hadn't meant to ignore them. In her paralysis, she really hadn't heard their questions.

Outside the room: giggles and talk. She caught a glimpse of tight smiles hanging with authority before they ushered her into a colossal, ornate hallway.

Some talk of a holiday. And the last of the visitors were escorted away. Perhaps had they not left, had Lagoa das Sete Cidades not been beckoning them so, Lauren wouldn't have been haunted with the sternness of their bidding.

And maybe she would have been spared the knotted switch (dual knotted switches, in fact; equal in the act of stinging her legs and tickling her thighs beneath her green-and-red plaid skirt).

And the paddle to follow.

Through the closing crack of the door, the indifference in her absconding father's face.

And the ordeals that birthed her night terrors.

The sky above the mountain was a light golden hue, but the sky rolling toward her—the clouds tumbling in boastful billows—were overcast. A nearly black purple.

They were growing darker. And quickly. An inky, grainy gloom spread inward in rumbles toward the mountain, both guising and hinting at an undercurrent of finality in the hellish avalanche.

Lauren felt no comfort in the quiet or in her repair, signified by the smooth scar on her abdomen. Her hands peddled down her sides, feeling the restoration, sensing the competency of her almost-surrogate body.

As something—no, someone—broke into sight, she was consumed by fatigue, exhaustion from the constant terrors. A blur loomed—a remote form wherefrom the darkness converged—and thoughts of rage and despair gamboled at her expense. She felt even wearier than before.

Not her body but her soul.

The dark cavalcade escorted a ghostly being, near imperceptible with the distance. Ivory robes and a pearl-white body. The contrast between the clouds and the figure was eerie.

She didn't know where she was. How she had gotten here. If she had died, which she sensed was somehow the case, what would be next? No answers assembled, so the inquiries fluttered out as they drifted in.

All but one.

And she was heavy with the question.

Why help—the help she would have given without hesitation to whomever she could—was so rarely given to her.

Copper clouds ebbed into the purple-black skies. And the stump nearly swayed.

Footprints like soot. The calloused ground beneath them had shifted.

Spikes splintered. Even the vines that tried to dissuade onlookers from any attempt to unhinge the shrine had frayed.

They hung depressingly, keen to break or be chopped and released of the burden of bracing the failing altar. Charred, but no smoke hung on its embers.

Everything was soundless and still.

And in the barbed entanglement, the slate bled.

ACKNOWLEDGMENTS

I wish to express my gratitude to those instrumental in the creation of this story:

Josh. For feeding our imaginations when we needed it most. And for coming up with ideas for stories since we were six. At the mobile home.

Rosebud. The first little lady I wanted to protect.

Aubrey. For being the first person to stomach this story and for the helpful honesty throughout many rewrites.

Todd. For taking the time to re-read my drafts more times than I know. My favorite masochist. And for advice, whether taken or foolishly ignored.

And to Mandy, Emily, and Micah: All my love

www.ingramcontent.com/pod-product-compliance
Lightning Source LLC
Chambersburg PA
CBHW020353130626
46549CB00006B/2281